An Unexpected Bride

Brides of Brighton Book 5

ASHTYN NEWBOLD

Copyright © 2019 by Ashtyn Newbold
All rights reserved.

No part of this book may be reproduced in any form whatsoever, whether by graphic, visual, electronic, film, microfilm, tape recording, or any other means, without prior written permission of the publisher, except in the case of brief passages embodied in critical reviews and articles.

This is a work of fiction. The characters, names, incidents, places and dialogue are products of the author's imaginations and are not to be construed as real. Any resemblance of characters to any person, living or dead, is purely coincidental.

ISBN 13: 9781075448751

Front cover design by Blue Water Books

For all the lights in my life

Chapter 1

WORTHING, ENGLAND, 1818

Five tiny fingers curled around Eleanor's wrist, and she looked down to see two round blue eyes, their dark lashes casting shadows over rosy cheeks. Eleanor knew the look on her son's face—she knew the pressure of his grip, the quiver of his chin, and the tenseness of his small frame.

"Not to worry, little one," she whispered, smoothing away his dark curls. "We are almost home."

"Home?" Arthur asked.

"Yes, home. The place where we can be safe and happy." *Safe and happy.* Eleanor drew a shuddering breath as their coach rolled over the path that passed through Worthing, a town she knew to be just ten miles from Brighton. Brighton was *home*.

"Are Papa and Grandpapa home?" Arthur stared out the window at the unfamiliar land, the distant ocean, the smooth, predictable landscape, and the manicured vegetation. Sunlight touched everything from the rooftops of houses with flowers sprouting from their gardens to the curve of Arthur's cheeks. He had hardly known anything but rocky ground, prickly moors, dark, stormy skies, and fierce wind.

"No, no," Eleanor said. "We need never see Papa and Grandpapa again." She wrapped her arm around Arthur's shoulders, and he slid down in his seat, resting his head in her lap. She swallowed, closing her eyes. Her legs shook, and she hoped Arthur couldn't feel it. He could never know that she was afraid too. "You will meet your Uncle Adam." Eleanor's voice broke with her brother's name.

Arthur turned his face up to hers. Hesitant, uncertain.

"Adam is kind, just like my father was." She blinked hard. Arthur had never seen her cry, and he never would. A beacon of strength was more comforting than reassuring words and promises.

She couldn't imagine what her father must have been feeling when he died, knowing that he would never see his daughter again. Adam had written to her saying that her father had succumbed to his illness shortly after she had been taken to Scotland—shortly after Mr. Quinton had forced her to marry him and forced her to write lies in her letters home to her family. *I am safe*, she had said. *I am happy. I love Mr. Quinton.*

How could she love the man that had torn her from her life in Brighton? Torn her from the protection and care of her brother and dying father? The thought that she had once loved Mr. Quinton sent disbelief scratching over her heart. If what she had once felt for Mr. Quinton was love, then she wanted no part of it. Love deceived, destroyed, and hurt everything in its path. Her heart had blinded her to what Mr. Quinton truly was all along—a monster in disguise. Her father had seen his true nature, but she had not believed him until it was too late.

She forced air in and out of her lungs, slow and steady. Mr. Quinton could not hurt her and Arthur again. He was dead. Her late husband's father, the elder Mr. Quinton, however, was not.

Eleanor began humming the song she often sang to Arthur in the silence of night and in the early hours of the morning.

"Sing, Mama," he said.

She brushed her fingers through his hair as she sang in a quiet voice.

Hush, rest your head
The rain will end
The cracks will mend
The clouds will part
Rest aching hearts.

Hush, close your eyes
The sun will rise
The robin sings
Of happy things
Of days ahead.

Hush, fall asleep
The past we'll keep
Let future reap
A spring to hold
A joy like gold

As she sang, Arthur visibly relaxed, his hands loosening on her wrist, his eyelids fluttering closed. They had been traveling for seven days, staying at various inns between Northumberland and Brighton. Eleanor counted the hours of travel as steps toward freedom, but she still could not banish the feeling that she was being followed. Chased. Her throat grew dry and her hands shook.

The coach continued on as Arthur slept on her lap. She checked the coins in her reticule, hoping she had what she needed to pay the coachman. She had brought all the money she had on her journey home, and she feared it would not be enough.

The uneven road turned Eleanor's stomach to knots, but Arthur's heavy breathing told her that he was still asleep. Summer rain began falling heavily, splashing on the windows in large droplets. In the distance, down the plush hill from the dirt path, Eleanor could see a small estate. It was two stories tall, with browned-butter stone, large windows, manicured gardens, and beautiful oak doors. She stared at the house, slightly blurred past sheets of rain. Standing firm and alone amid a storm, the house felt very much like a beacon of its own—a beacon of strength and hope.

With a lurch, the coach suddenly stopped. It teetered off balance for a brief second, and Eleanor clutched Arthur to keep him from falling off the seat. The horses brayed, and the coach slid to the left before falling completely still.

Eleanor straightened in alarm, her gaze darting out the window. Had highwaymen stopped their coach? In the light of day? Her heart hammered. Or had her late husband's father, the elder Mr. Quinton, discovered his son, motionless and dead, and come to find her and Arthur?

"Mama." His little voice sounded more curious than afraid. "Are we home?"

She put a finger to her lips, craning her neck out the window again. Just as she did, the coach door flew open. She stifled a shriek, pulling Arthur to her chest. Fully expecting to see the robust figure of the elder Mr. Quinton, or even a masked highwayman, she was relieved to see the extremely slender form and bald head of their hired coachman, Mr. Fifett. Rain dripped down his face, catching in the sparse dark mustache above his lip. "My apologies, ma'am, but I'm afraid we've fallen upon a spot of mud. 'Twill take but a short moment to be on our way."

She swallowed past her dry throat so she could speak. Misty air blew into the coach, sending shivers over her arms. She tugged at her gloves. "That is no problem at all." Considering what her imagination had conjured about their sudden halting, she was quite relieved to hear that it was only the result of a little mud.

Mr. Fifett shifted, his boots sinking into the mud as well. "I'm afraid I must ask that you and your boy step outside for a moment while I push the coach out of the mud. I doubt I could budge it with the weight of the both of you."

She eyed his slender arms, agreeing wholeheartedly with his assessment.

"Oh." Eleanor glanced at the pouring rain again. "Yes, of course." She lifted her bonnet off her black curls, setting it atop Arthur's head. The wide brim would protect him well from the rain. It was the width of his shoulders, at least.

She took the coachman's hand, stepping down to the ground before reaching inside to pick up Arthur. He wrapped his arms around her neck, tipping his head up to look at the storm. She followed his gaze to the charcoal clouds where they twisted in the sky, wringing out moisture like a wet cloth. The moment she stepped away from the coach, warm rain plummeted down, soaking through her hair and dress. Her feet sank into the mud as she walked several steps back. She blinked against the water in her eyes.

"Twill take a short moment, that is all," The coachman half-shouted over the pounding rain. He slogged around to the other side of the coach, examining each wheel to find the one that was stuck.

"I believe it is this one here," Eleanor said, pointing at the nearest wheel, the front right, buried deep in unrelenting mud.

"Ah, yes."

To Eleanor's surprise, Mr. Fifett dropped to his knees with a splash, rolling up his sleeves to his knobbed elbows. He dug around the wheel with his fingertips, picking up miniscule amounts of mud. At this rate, it would not take a *short moment*.

She continued standing in the rain, holding Arthur close. The thought of him catching a cold terrified her. The last time he had fallen ill he had narrowly survived. The bonnet shielded his head well from the rain, but his clothing was soaked, and the air grew colder by the minute. She felt as if she were still in Northumberland. There had been many occasions that she had confined herself to the house to avoid rain such as this. She had to remind herself that she was not there any longer, not afraid, not trapped, and certainly not weak.

"Sir, please allow me to help you."

The coachman lifted his head. What could only have been a mixture of rain and sweat poured down his red face. He hesitated. "Oh, no, ma'am, I mustn't employ a lady's assistance."

"I am already soaked, sir. I would like to help so I may take my son out of this weather as soon as possible." She held his gaze. When he didn't react, she set Arthur down several feet away and marched to the back of the coach. She took hold of the back corner and dug her feet into the mud as she pushed with all the energy she possessed. She heaved her body weight forward, her arms shaking with exertion as she tried to budge the coach. It didn't move.

She walked around to the coachman, who stared at her as if she had descended from another world. He held a scant handful of mud in each palm.

"Perhaps I might dry digging, and you push?" she suggested.

He nodded. When he stood, she saw that the entirety of his knee breeches were covered in mud, his arms the same, all the way up to the elbows. She swallowed, picking up her skirts with one hand as she bent over the wheel. She sunk her hands into the wet earth, making a sliding and scooping motion to free an armful of mud. Working quickly, she created a ditch around the wheel as well as a slope in front of it, so the horses could easily pull the wheel up and forward. The horses shifted, sending a splash of mud toward her face. She blinked hard against the water and mud that now dripped down her cheeks and eyelids.

"May I be of assistance?" Another voice came from behind, a deep baritone—a voice that made the coachman's sound quite childish in comparison.

Eleanor turned, glancing up to see the man who had spoken. He appeared to have addressed the coachman, but he stared down at Eleanor with concern, a set of piercing blue eyes meeting hers through sheets of heavy rain. He looked familiar, though she could not quite place him.

His clothing too was soaked, water dripping off the brim of his hat. He extended one hand toward her, and she took it hesitantly. The man pulled her to her feet, taking in her appearance with steady flicks of his gaze. His eyes flashed with recognition. "Miss Claridge?"

She drew a quick breath as she studied the man's face in closer proximity. How did he know her? He did look very familiar. As she took in his blue eyes and golden blond hair, she determined that he could only be the younger Beaumont son, a family she had grown up near in Brighton. What was Mr. Beaumont doing in Worthing? She had been briefly acquainted with Lord Ramsbury, the eldest Beaumont son, five years before. She could vaguely recall meeting this man as well. There was no mistaking the intensity of both men's gazes, the striking blue and the inarguable attention.

Before she could respond, Mr. Beaumont shrugged out of his jacket, draping it over her head and shoulders. She gripped the lapels, grateful for the shield from the rain. She stepped back to Arthur's side. He clung to her skirts.

With Mr. Beaumont's help, the coach was free within a minute, rolling past the deep mud to much more steady ground. Eleanor's arms shook from the recent exertion of digging, and Arthur trembled in the cold beside her.

"I thank you most ardently, good sir." Mr. Fifett shook Mr. Beaumont's hand before turning back toward Eleanor. "Shall we be on our way?"

She picked up her skirts with one hand, the weight of the water and mud that had soaked through causing them to drag on the ground. Arthur grasped her other hand as they walked back toward the coach. She paused beside Mr. Beaumont, handing his jacket back to him. "Thank you," she said, her voice quiet.

She could only imagine what Mr. Beaumont thought of her. When she had disappeared five years before, the entire town of Brighton had likely been curious as to her whereabouts. Then she had written to her father, telling him of her elopement, and her reputation had surely crumbled. More likely than not, Mr. Beaumont was thinking all sorts of disdainful things about her. She stood, uncomfortable under his study.

The rain had softened to a trickle, the clouds parting above them. The timing was impeccable.

"Is it really you, Miss Claridge?" Mr. Beaumont asked. "Or…my apologies, what shall I call you now?"

He was referring to her married name. The name she would now always bear, a reminder of the wicked man she had once loved. "Mrs. Quinton," she said. She wanted to say more, but fear stopped the words in her throat. What would Mr. Beaumont do if he learned her husband was dead, and she was fleeing from her home in the North?

He took her hand and helped her into the coach, lifting Arthur in beside her. Mr. Beaumont's expression was all curiosity and concern. "Is this your son?"

"Yes," she said.

"And what shall I call him?"

"Arthur."

A smile crossed Mr. Beaumont's face for the first time, a gentle upturn of his lips. "How great it is to meet you, Arthur."

Eleanor cast her gaze down to her son, who had nestled his face into her arm, hiding from Mr. Beaumont's view. "He is shy, that is all," she said, though it was not entirely true. Arthur had every reason to fear unfamiliar men. Even those that should have been most safe, secure, and trustworthy had given him great cause to fear. His father and grandfather most of all.

Mr. Beaumont crossed his arms, glancing at the coachman, who had reclaimed his seat, before returning his gaze back to Eleanor. "Are you bound for Brighton?"

She nodded. Would he not let them leave? She was quite uncomfortable and wet, and her stomach had begun squeezing with pangs of hunger. And she hated to see Arthur suffer, as wet and cold as he was. She needed to get him to Brighton quickly, where he could warm up by a fire.

"That is still ten miles away," Mr. Beaumont said.

Precisely. Eleanor wished to remain polite, but her patience was running thin. "Yes, so we must be on our way."

"You intend to travel for another hour in your current state?" He shook his head. "I admire your resilience, Mrs. Quinton." A soft smile. "My estate is just there, beyond the hill. I insist that you and your son come for a short time to change into warm, dry clothing and eat before taking the remainder of your trip."

Eleanor followed his gaze out to the house she had noticed before the coach had gotten stuck. Free from the rain, the lines and curves of the house came into clear focus. She met Mr. Beaumont's eyes, and the pleading there combined with Arthur's shivering gave her little choice in the matter. "Very well. That is very kind of you."

He nodded, walking toward the front of the coach. He offered Mr. Fifett the same courtesy, to which he heartily agreed.

Mr. Beaumont stepped into the coach, taking a seat across from Eleanor and Arthur, closing the door behind him. The coach began rolling forward before turning around, heading back in the direction of Mr. Beaumont's estate. Eleanor kept her gaze fixed on her lap, stroking her fingertips over Arthur's hair. She stole a glance at his face, where his eyes lay fixed on Mr. Beaumont.

"Are you visiting your brother in Brighton?" The baritone voice asked.

Eleanor glanced up. "Yes." Another pang of grief struck her as she thought of her father, and how she would never see him again. The grief was muddled with guilt over the pain she must have caused him by leaving with Mr. Quinton. She tried to assure herself that the fault was not her own, but the assurances she gave herself always became lost in the harsh, drunken tones of her late husband's voice. She pressed away the sounds that haunted her mind, focusing on the man in front of her. Could Mr. Beaumont be trusted? She pulled Arthur closer.

Mr. Beaumont gave another of his small smiles, the expression still mingled with deep curiosity. "When were you last in Brighton?"

Her fingers twitched on her skirts. "Five years ago."

"Five years?" His voice remained polite and respectful but carried a tone of disbelief. "Has your brother not been acquainted with Arthur? Your boy cannot be older than four."

"No." Her breathing had increased in rate, but she tried to appear nonchalant. "I have been living near the border of Scotland. It is quite a long journey back to Brighton." She could not possibly tell Mr. Beaumont that the only reason she had not come fleeing back long ago was because her husband would not allow it. But he could not stop her now, and that was the only reason she was on this coach. Her heart pounded and she closed her eyes against a surge of nausea and unpleasant memories.

When she opened her eyes again, she found Mr. Beaumont watching her carefully. He had the most curious stare she had ever encountered. She ought to have been uncomfortable with his intense study, but there was nothing menacing about it. Nothing unsettling or chilling. He simply watched her as if he was afraid she would faint or shrink or disappear at any moment. She dearly hoped he had no more questions for her.

"Why did your husband not accompany you?" he asked. "How could he send his wife and son on such a long journey alone, and on a hired coach, no less?"

Blast the man for all his questions. She exhaled sharply, smoothing her palm over Arthur's arm. In her youth, she had been taught that honesty was a virtue to always uphold, no matter the circumstances. Her father had been an advocate of honesty and always spoke freely. But telling the truth now would result in unfathomable consequences. How great of lengths was she willing to take to protect Arthur? A lie danced on the tip of her tongue, and she had little choice but to set it free. "My husband was deterred with business, sir. He was so kind as to allow Arthur and I to take a trip while he was away so we would not be so bored at home in his absence."

She hoped Arthur did not fully understand her words. She knew his shy nature to be enough to keep him from contradicting her, but she did not want to teach him that lying was acceptable. At least not under normal circumstances. She and Arthur's circumstances, of course, were far from normal.

Mr. Beaumont gave a small nod. "I see. Aside from the recent storm, have your travels been comfortable?"

"Yes, quite."

"I am glad to hear that."

She heard the smile in his voice, warm and strangely

comforting. She had forgotten what a kind voice sounded like. She did not have to cringe when she heard his inhale, as he drew air into his lungs to fuel his next statement. She did not have to cover Arthur's ears against angry shouting and unholy words. She knew Henry Beaumont to be a respectable man, at least by his reputation. His brother, Lord Ramsbury, had been a notorious flirt, and had even flirted with Eleanor on more than one occasion. She had never taken it seriously. She was glad to pretend she was still married, if only to thwart unwelcome attention from gentlemen. If Henry Beaumont was anything like his older brother, then she was happy to lie and tell him her husband was alive. She wanted nothing to do with men ever again. The only man she could trust was her brother, Adam.

The coachman led the horses down a narrow stone path, one that led directly to Mr. Beaumont's front property. Eleanor paused to admire the house again, taking in the beauty of the architecture and cleanliness of the grounds. She almost sighed. She had missed the southern coast of England. The neat, orderly, and predictable environment brought her more comfort than anything else. She felt as if she were finally in control of something again.

Now all she had to do was endure her meal with Mr. Beaumont, and she would be one step closer to home.

Chapter 2

When the coach stopped in the drive, Mr. Beaumont helped Eleanor and Arthur down. The coachman followed as they were led toward the front steps. The sky still held a hint of grey, but the storm had almost completely cleared, and the earth smelled fresh and cleansed, as if the sky had just granted it a new beginning. The grass was soggy and pliant beneath her boots. She could not possibly become wetter than she already was, so she didn't mind it.

As they walked through the front doors, the housekeeper, butler, and two footmen stood at attention.

"What a lovely, home you have," Mr. Fifett said, his voice echoing under the lofty ceiling of the entry hall.

Mr. Beaumont thanked him before instructing the footmen to fetch Eleanor's things from the coach. She had managed to fit both hers and Arthur's possessions into one small trunk. She hoped she hadn't forgotten anything of great importance in her hurry to leave Northumberland.

Mr. Beaumont turned toward Eleanor, ushering a young maid forward. She curtsied.

"Mary will show you a guest room where she will help you and Arthur change into dry clothing," Mr. Beaumont said. "I will ask my cook to prepare a meal immediately."

Eleanor's stomach grumbled in answer to his words, quiet enough to escape Mr. Beaumont's notice, but not Arthur's. He grinned up at her. "I'm hungry too, Mama."

She smiled. "Mr. Beaumont has been very kind to provide us with a meal."

Arthur looked up their host, eyeing him with skepticism. His smile faded even as Mr. Beaumont gave him a broad grin.

The footmen returned with Eleanor's trunk, and she took Arthur's hand as they followed the young maid, Mary, up the stairs. Eleanor tried not to let her muddy skirts drag on the fine marble. It had been so long since she had been in such a lovely house. She swept her gaze over her surroundings, in awe over the fine architecture and decoration of the home.

Mary worked quickly, washing and brushing through Eleanor's tangled, muddy hair. She did the same for Arthur. After they were changed into dry, warm clothing, they met Mr. Beaumont downstairs, where he had started a fire in the drawing room.

Mr. Beaumont offered Eleanor and Arthur each their own comfortable chair, and she sat down. Eleanor sighed as the warmth that radiated from the flames absorbed moisture off her face and hair. So enjoyable was the sensation, that she nearly forgot that Mr. Beaumont still sat beside her and Arthur, watching her with the same unabashed curiosity as before.

"Are you feeling well?" he asked when she met his eyes.

"Much better."

He smiled, the warmth emitting from the expression almost greater than the warmth from the fire. Eleanor sat back in her chair, sudden emotion clawing at her throat. How had she been away from kindness for so long that she had forgotten what it felt like to be a recipient of it? Arthur sat forward on his chair, extending his hands toward the flames to warm them. She did not know where Mr. Fifett had gone, but she wished he were in the room. Perhaps then Mr. Beaumont would not direct all of his attention at her.

"You have a beautiful home," she said. "When did you move away from Brighton?"

Mr. Beaumont leaned his elbows on his knees, staring into the flames much like Arthur was doing. "When my father died four years ago, he was kind enough to leave me this estate. He left the estate in Brighton as well as the earldom to my elder brother, as expected." A slight smile tugged on his lips. "He did threaten to disinherit my brother and hand over everything to me, but after seeing the effort my brother put forward to keep it, I am quite pleased with this arrangement."

Eleanor knew the brother he spoke of. "Your brother is Lord Ramsbury." She did not have a high opinion of the man. She once had, but that was before she married Mr. Quinton, a close friend of Lord Ramsbury's. What did it say about one's character to be friends with such a despicable man?

"He has taken on my father's title now, Lord Coventry, though I simply call him Edward." Mr. Beaumont smiled again, a twinkling that reached his eyes. Eleanor could see a stark resemblance between the brothers in their eyes, golden blond hair, and broad stature. But Mr. Beaumont's countenance was softer somehow, more genuine and youthful, especially with the shadows and highlights of the nearby fire reflecting off his features. She noted the smoothness of his brow and cheek, finished with a solid jaw and straight nose. He had a remarkably handsome face, but above all, it was a kind face, and that was what made it the most remarkable.

She realized how long she had been staring at him, quickly turning her gaze toward Arthur. "Your brother was—is a friend of my husband's."

Mr. Beaumont nodded, slow and deliberate. "Yes. I believe Edward caused a quarrel between himself and your brother Adam when he kept your location secret after your marriage."

Her elopement had surely been the talk of Brighton once it had been discovered. Eleanor had not known that Mr. Quinton had confided in anyone about the elopement. Had he told his confidants that it was a kidnapping? She had not realized that Mr. Quinton's friendship with Lord Ramsbury had run so deep. Mr. Quinton had demanded that she convince two of her own friends that she was happily eloping at Gretna Green, so as to give her family every reason to believe the truth of her letter that explained her happiness.

She shook off the emotion that burned in her chest at the thought of the letter. She had read it over countless times, making corrections at Mr. Quinton's demand. She pictured the fresh parchment, the wax seal, and the dirt on the edges where she had creased it and unfolded it again and again. It was a letter filled with lies.

Dear Papa,

There is little I can say to you in the way of apology, for I know I do not deserve your forgiveness, nor do I ask for it. I also do not ask for your understanding, but only that you receive this missive and know that I am alive, and I am happy. I write now as I ride to London, where I will marry Mr. William Quinton. I love Mr. Quinton, and I know he will bring me exceeding happiness. Knowing that you did not approve of him and would never endorse the match, I aspired to escape in secret. My reputation will be safe as well as the Claridge name, not to worry. Suspecting you or perhaps Adam may follow me to London, I was forced to keep my departure a secret, as was Mr. Quinton, until we had secured our marriage.

I confided in but two trusted friends, Miss Darby and Miss Reed. Please do not blame them for fulfilling their promise of silence to me. Mr. Quinton confided in one man of the regiment, and another man of his acquaintance.

I shall think of you and Adam often. Please do not come searching for me, for I do not wish to return to Brighton. I regret the worry and unease I have caused you, and wish you all the best in your recovery to good health. I cannot give you the address in which I will receive your letters, but I will promise to write you upon occasion.

With love and sincerity,

Eleanor

"I hope your brother does not still harbor any ill feelings toward my brother," Mr. Beaumont said, obstructing her thoughts. "Although if he does, I do not blame him for it."

Eleanor knew that her husband had not given Lord

Ramsbury their true location, so it would not have helped even if he had told Adam the truth of where she was. After reading the letter she sent, Adam likely never came searching for her anyway. She could not help but feel that he hated her now. He believed that she had abandoned him and their father.

Taking a deep breath, she reminded herself that she would soon be able to explain it all to him.

"I have not written to Adam in years, so I do not know his opinion of your brother." Eleanor realized the mistake of her words the moment she spoke them—the moment she saw the crease in Mr. Beaumont's brow.

"What has stopped you from writing?"

"Postage was an expense we simply could not afford."

Mr. Beaumont's brow tightened further. His voice remained soft, but deeply inquisitive. "Yet you could afford such a long journey by hired coach?"

She still feared she couldn't afford to pay Mr. Fifett. Shifting in her chair, she told yet another lie. "Well, Mr. Quinton has been planning this trip for us for a long while and has set aside the needed funds."

Mr. Beaumont nodded, though she suspected he was not entirely convinced. Was she truly so terrible a liar? "I am glad you were able to take the trip," he said. "Your brother will be very happy to see you after so long a time."

Mr. Beaumont moved his gaze to Arthur before shifting his chair abruptly closer. She instinctively clutched Arthur's arm. Mr. Beaumont's gaze flicked to hers with concern. Her grip loosened. What was she thinking? Mr. Beaumont was not threatening. He would not hurt her or Arthur. She allowed her heartbeat to slow as Mr. Beaumont reached into his jacket, withdrawing a tiny seashell. He slowly extended his hand to Arthur, offering the shell to him. "When I was a young boy, I collected seashells. To this day I cannot ignore a beautiful shell when I see it on the beach. I found this one this morning. Would you like to have it?"

Eleanor craned her neck to see Arthur's expression. He glanced at her for approval. She nodded toward the shell, smiling to give him courage. In one quick swipe, Arthur took the shell from Mr. Beaumont's palm.

He chuckled. "He is a shy one, isn't he?"

Eleanor laughed, but it came off weak. "He is, indeed."

A few minutes later, a maid came in the drawing room with several hot trays of food. Mr. Fifett joined them at the card table in a set of dry clothing, where they sat down to dine. Mr. Beaumont smiled. "I know this is a strange place to eat, but I did not wish to take you away from the warmth of the fire. I hope you find this arrangement comfortable enough."

"This is perfect, thank you." Eleanor's mouth watered at the aromas that wafted up from the silver platters. Fresh bread, butter, jam, and cheese were arranged on one tray, and the other held fruit and sliced ham. After arranging a plate for Arthur, she gathered food onto her own. As she ate, gratitude surged in her heart for the generosity of a near stranger.

"Do you live alone here?" The coachman asked Mr. Beaumont. Eleanor had not thought to ask such a question. She had not seen any evidence of a wife or children, but she supposed they could be out visiting neighbors or in the nursery.

"Yes, it is just me," Mr. Beaumont said. "The neighborhood is very kind to call on me often, so I am not forced to always be in solitude. I visit my family in Brighton as frequently as I am able."

Mr. Fifett smiled. Eleanor watched with fascination as he managed to mix nearly every food item on the platter—grapes, jam, butter, ham, and cheese, placing it between two thick slices of bread. He took a large bite, chewing loudly. His eyebrows lifted in delight as he chewed. "Certainly they would not hesitate to call on such a generous and kind acquaintance." Mr. Fifett's voice came out muffled, jam oozing out the corners of his mouth.

Eleanor could see the fascination and slight revulsion in Mr. Beaumont's eyes as he watched the coachman eat his concoction. But he hid it well behind a friendly smile. "My neighbors have been very welcoming, yes."

Before he had swallowed the first, Mr. Fifett took a second bite. Mr. Beaumont's eyes widened ever so slightly. For a man of such a slight frame, Eleanor was thoroughly surprised that the coachman could eat so much.

The coachman gave a slow nod as he took yet another bite, his words entirely intelligible. "I imuffuff choo reciffs muffug foo fmuffle."

Henry's eyes met Eleanor's briefly, a smile dancing in them. She pressed down her own smile, glancing at Arthur, who stared at the coachman with his own fascination. She hoped he would not begin to imitate Mr. Fifett's dining manners.

"Pardon me?" Mr. Beaumont asked.

With one forceful swallow, the coachman cleared his throat. "I imagine you receive many visitors just for the marvelous food you offer." He licked his fingers before taking a swig from his goblet. "It is quite marvelous indeed."

Mr. Beaumont grinned, a wide smile that Eleanor guessed he had been suppressing for several minutes. "Even if that is their only reason for visiting, I am still happy to receive them. Better that than to be alone all of my days. I have lived here four years now."

"Why have you not married?"

Eleanor was shocked by both the coachman's prodding questions, and Henry's calm reaction to them.

"I hope to marry only for the most ardent love and affection. Such a thing is difficult to find."

Eleanor studied his face. Mr. Beaumont would be searching forever if he hoped to find such a thing. She did not know men had such ambitions as love. Mr. Quinton certainly hadn't.

"Indeed, very difficult." The coachman chuckled, finishing the enormous portion of what remained on his tray in one bite. Eleanor kept her eyes fixed on Mr. Beaumont's face as he smiled again. He tipped his chin downward, as if hoping to hide the expression in the folds of his cravat.

Mr. Fifett turned toward Eleanor. "I'm afraid my schedule will not allow for a long delay. We must be on the road again as soon as possible."

Eleanor nodded, catching Mr. Beaumont's gaze. "Thank you very much for your hospitality."

He watched her stand, rising as well. "It was my pleasure, Mrs. Quinton."

She felt his gaze on her face for a long moment as she gathered Arthur into her arms. He was quite small for his age, so it was no trouble to carry him. She dreaded the day he became too heavy to carry. She feared letting him walk on his own feet and wander away from her side too often. Taking a deep breath, she cast Mr. Beaumont one last smile and nod before exiting through the drawing room door. She hoped he hadn't suspected the truth of her situation. Had he been aware that she was lying?

"Ah, what a delicious meal, that was," the coachman said as they walked back to the coach and stepped inside.

With what remained of the drive to Brighton, Eleanor heard those words on multiple occasions, and many other variations of praise over Mr. Beaumont's meal. But all Eleanor could seem to recall of the event was Mr. Beaumont's kindness and striking blue eyes.

Arthur turned his new seashell over in his hands repeatedly as the coach moved smoothly down the road toward Brighton.

Chapter 3

The smell of Brighton was one Eleanor would always remember. She had lived near the sea all of her life, whether it was the sea on the northern tip of England, or the sea on the southern. The Brighton coast was different. It smelled of salt and mist and a fresh cleanliness that reminded her of peace and belonging. No matter what Mr. Quinton had tried to convince her to believe, she did not leave Brighton willingly. She never would have, and she never would again.

She stepped out of the carriage where it had stopped in front of her childhood home. She fumbled through her reticule, withdrawing the last of her coins. She approached Mr. Fifett, opening her palm. Her heart pounded. Would it be enough?

His eyes fell on the coins, and he shook his head. "No, ma'am. Mr. Beaumont has already paid your way."

"Pardon me?" She must have heard him incorrectly.

"The cost of your journey has been paid in its entirety by Mr. Beaumont. He is a very generous man, indeed."

Eleanor could scarcely believe it. What had she done to deserve such kindness? Mr. Beaumont did not know her. He did not owe her anything. How could she ever thank him? Hot tears burned behind her eyes, sending tightness down her throat. Her heart warmed, her opinion of Mr. Beaumont growing in positivity.

She took Arthur's hand, looking up toward the house in front of them. Nothing had changed—the house appeared as it had the day she left. She stepped onto the neat grass. The joyful emotion that pulsed through her was suddenly overcome by fear. Would Adam still want her here? Would he resent her? Would he understand? In the five years that she had been apart from her brother, she had lost a sense of familiarity with his character. She remembered his devotion and generosity, but what if he had changed? She certainly had.

Pushing aside her fear, she took one step, then another, closer to the front door. With a deep breath of fortitude, she struck the wood three times. The sound echoed through the air, pounding against her aching skull. Arthur squeezed her hand tighter as the door swung open.

The same butler that had greeted her on many occasions as a child stood in the doorway. He too appeared very much the same, but slightly older. His eyes flashed with recognition as he took in her face. Before the stunned butler could utter a word, Eleanor cleared her throat.

"Is Adam here?" she asked.

He nodded, stepping aside for her to enter. "He was on his way out for a ride with his wife, but I believe he is still in the nursery."

Eleanor felt another wave of grief. *Wife? Nursery?* Mr.

Quinton had taken her away from her family for long enough to miss her brother's wedding? The birth of his child? The emotion in her chest rose and fell in waves, growing stronger with each pulse. She wiped the perspiration from her palms on her skirts before picking Arthur up and propping him on her hip. The butler seemed to recover from his shock for long enough to speak. "What has brought you back to Brighton? Why are you here? The master is not expecting you."

The disdain in his voice was heavy and direct. He, much like everyone in Brighton, still believed her departure to have been voluntary, selfish, and cruel. She swallowed, reminding herself that this disdain was something she would have to grow accustomed to.

"I should think it is quite obvious that I have come to visit my brother." She cast the butler a quick glance before stepping forward with forced confidence. "Shall I wait for him in the drawing room?"

The butler nodded, a quick tip of his head. "I will inform him of your arrival."

Eleanor thanked him before turning the corner to where she knew she would find the drawing room. She took in the walls, the side tables in the entry, and the chandelier above, a wistful feeling pinching her heart.

When she entered the drawing room, she was surprised to find a woman sitting in a nearby chair. The moment the door opened, the woman turned around with a gasp, her blonde curls tight and bouncy as they framed her round, rosy face. "You nearly frightened me to death!" she exclaimed before fully taking in Eleanor's appearance. The moment the woman saw her, the playful expression of fear on her face slackened. "Oh, my apologies, I thought you were my niece, Amelia."

Eleanor stared at her. The woman looked much too old to be Adam's wife. Her hand pressed against her chest as she gave a boisterous laugh. "I assure you, you did not truly frighten me to near *death*, I was only exaggerating as I always do. It is one of my most renowned qualities." The woman's pale blue eyes danced as she spoke, giving life and youth to the wrinkles around her smile.

"Does your niece live here?" Eleanor asked.

The woman watched her carefully as she carried Arthur to the sofa. Eleanor sat down, studying the details of the room. It had been redecorated, a task she could likely credit Adam's wife for.

"Why, yes, she does indeed. My niece is the mistress of this home, in fact." She grinned with pride before offering her own introduction. "My name is Margaret Buxton. I am visiting for the summer from Nottingham. I come as often as I am able to take the cure, you see. The healing qualities of the Brighton waters have served my leg quite nicely over the years." She tapped her cane that rested against the edge of her chair. "I hardly need this any longer." She beamed. "Forgive me, I am prattling on about things you do not care to hear." She tipped her head to the side. "I daresay I have not seen you here before."

Eleanor hoped that Adam's wife was as instantly likable as this woman. There was something about the woman's familiar and friendly disposition that gave instant ease to Eleanor's fear. "I have not been here in several years. I am Adam's sister Eleanor. It is a pleasure to meet you."

The woman gave a loud gasp, making both Eleanor and Arthur jump.

"Oh! Oooh!" The woman stood up, fanning her face with one hand and holding her cane in the other, bustling around the room as if she did not know which direction to travel. She stopped in front of Eleanor, her eyes rounder than the saucers on the tea table. "You are Eleanor?"

"I am indeed." Eleanor couldn't prevent her own expression from mirroring the woman's surprise.

"You have returned to Brighton!"

"Yes—"

"Oh, Adam will be so very pleased." The woman's pacing had increased in rate, and Eleanor noticed a distinct limp to her gait. She paused by the pianoforte to rub her hip. "I am so very pleased to meet you." The woman smiled broadly. "We are practically family, after all. I have known you all this time as Adam's sister Eleanor, the one who disappeared five years ago, the first summer I came to Brighton. How fortuitous that I was here visiting my niece when you decided to make your return. Oh, I do love a good dose of excitement and intrigue." She seemed to remember something very important, her bright blue eyes darting to the door. "I must fetch Adam straight away!"

She started toward the door, limping as she went. When she reached the doorframe, she turned to Eleanor with a look that was somewhat stern, a sharp contrast to her previous joviality. "Stay there. Please do not run off again."

Eleanor nodded, too shocked to speak. Margaret bustled out the door, muttering a string of excited and flustered words as she went.

Arthur tipped his head up to look at Eleanor, his tiny lips pinched in a frown. "Who was that?"

Eleanor had never met a more energetic woman above the age of fifty as this woman appeared to be. "That was our new friend."

Arthur stared at the door, his brows contracting.

Minutes later, the door swung open again. Adam stepped over the threshold, his dark hair neater than Eleanor remembered it, his eyes sharp and blue and filled with tears. "Eleanor?"

She stood, leaving Arthur sitting on the sofa behind her. She hadn't expected the surge of emotion that gripped her in that moment, firm and unyielding. She met her brother in the middle of the room, falling into his outstretched arms. Tears stung and burned on her eyes, but she didn't let them fall. Relief stronger than any she had ever felt washed over her in repetitive waves as Adam held her. She was finally home. She was finally safe. But her ruse was not over.

She stepped back, taking a deep, collective breath.

"Where have you been?" Adam asked, searching her face as if attempting to find the answer there before she could say it aloud.

"I have been in Northumberland."

"I searched for you in London. I could find no trace of you." Adam's brows were drawn together, a certain reservation in his expression. "Why did you never write? Why did you stay away for so long?"

She had expected to be assailed with questions, so she had spent much of the drive to Brighton crafting the answers in her mind. She did not know why she felt the need to lie. She could trust Adam! What was she so afraid of?

Still, the lies came pouring out. "I was grieving papa's death on my own for so long, and I felt to speak to you would intensify my grief. When my son was born, I became quite busy. I suppose I became enamored with my new life, and I forgot to keep myself tied to my old one." As heartless as the words sounded, she couldn't help but speak them.

Adam glanced behind her to the sofa where Arthur sat quietly, watching the exchange with curiosity and a touch of worry. Eleanor stepped away from Adam, taking Arthur by the hand and guiding him toward Adam. "This is your Uncle Adam." She watched Arthur surveying Adam, distrust evident in his eyes. He glanced at Eleanor's face for reassurance. She had always been told that she and Adam had a clear resemblance. Both their eyes were blue with a similar shape, and both had the same black hair. She hoped the similarity would give Arthur ease. She straightened her posture, addressing her brother. "This is my son, Arthur."

Adam smiled, leaning down for a closer look at him. "Good day, Arthur. It is a pleasure to meet you. I have a little girl of my own that must be very near to your age. She is your cousin." Adam met Eleanor's eyes. "Her name is Eleanor."

Eleanor's heart jumped, guilt flooding through her veins. She had to remind herself once again that it had not been her choice to leave. Yes, she had been foolish for trusting Mr. Quinton, but it was not her fault that she deserted her family, leading them to believe they would never see her again. She hated that it had caused such pain to Adam. "I'm sorry, Adam," she whispered. "I should never have left."

He stared at her, a look that was part awe and part frustration. "Why did you take so long to come visit? You might have at least told me where you were so I could visit you." His jaw tightened. "Or did your husband prevent it?"

Her skin bristled, her tightly locked secrets begging to be unveiled. She opened her mouth to speak but closed it again. What was she afraid of? Mr. Quinton was dead.

She could tell Adam he was dead without telling him what happened the day she left. She could keep *some* secrets. "My husband died."

"When?"

"Just before I came here."

Adam did not appear surprised to find little emotion in Eleanor's voice or expression. She could not force herself to act as if she grieved the man. "Did he leave you with a jointure? Any property?"

She shook her head. "I left very soon after his death, so I have not been informed. But it would be my instant assumption that no, he did not. I would be quite surprised to learn that he left me with anything." Standing beside her brother in the safe comfort of her home, she could not help but unleash at least one of her secrets. "I am certain he never cared for me," she whispered.

Adam's breathing grew quick, as if anger were pushing it out from his lungs. "What happened? I never entirely believed your letter. I couldn't believe that you would leave us with Father so ill. I never thought you capable of leaving at all, risking your reputation and our family's for a man that Father did not approve of. You loved Father, didn't you?"

"Yes," she whispered. "Very much."

Behind Adam's shoulder, Margaret and a younger woman slipped into the room. Adam turned at the sound of the door, ushering the young woman forward. Only when she reached his side did Eleanor see the little girl walking beside her, dressed in a pale pink dress, her light brown hair falling straight and long for a girl so young. She stared up at Eleanor with round, coffee colored eyes.

Adam took the woman's hand. "Eleanor, this is my wife, Amelia, and our daughter. We call her Ella."

Eleanor met the woman's intelligent brown eyes, smiling as much as she was able. The woman surveyed her in quick glances. Her face had a friendly warmth that could not be taught, a disposition similar to her aunt's. Underneath it, however, was the same curiosity and confusion that Eleanor had seen in every expression she had encountered—especially Mr. Beaumont's.

Amelia took Eleanor's hands. "I cannot believe you are here." Her voice carried a friendliness that matched her face. "I look forward to coming to know you, for I have heard such wonderful things from my husband."

Did Adam truly speak highly of her? How could he after what he believed she had done? "I did not know my brother married while I was away," Eleanor said, offering a smile. "I am so happy to meet you." Eleanor felt an instant connection with the woman and suspected they would become very dear friends. She hoped Arthur and his little cousin could become friends too. Arthur hadn't had the opportunity to spend time in the company of other young children. She glanced down at him. He watched little Ella with trepidation, holding fast to Eleanor's hand. She introduced him to Amelia and Ella, who both seemed quite pleased to make his acquaintance.

"He is positively adorable," Amelia said.

Adam touched Eleanor's shoulder, calling her attention back to him. "Please tell me what happened. Tell me the truth."

At the reminder of his earlier question, her stomach flipped. "I have already told you."

"I wish for the *truth*, Eleanor. I have been searching for it—for you—for five years now. I deserve to know."

Amelia nudged Adam's arm, giving him a look that was a gentle rebuke. "Eleanor has traveled far. We are all quite curious, but she and little Arthur must be quite fatigued and hungry."

Eleanor shook her head. "We just ate and rested in Worthing an hour ago. Do you know a Mr. Henry Beaumont? He offered us a few minutes to rest and eat on our journey. He was very kind."

Adam's jaw clenched yet again, and a look of pure vexation crossed his features. "Yes, I know the Beaumonts. I am not well acquainted with Henry, but I know his brother to be less than agreeable. He knew of your location and kept it from us. Even so, he must have given us the wrong location. I was never able to find you in London."

She debated again over whether or not she should tell her brother the truth in its entirety. What harm could it do? He was the only person she knew with certainty that she could trust. And her trust was not easily won. "I am told that Lord Ramsbury has changed a great deal in recent years."

"Did Mr. Henry Beaumont tell you this?" Adam asked, his eyebrows rising. "What has given you the idea that you can believe a word he says? Of course he would defend his brother."

"He was very kind."

"Kindness and charm are often a ruse meant to lure in the most naive. Is that what your husband did?"

Amelia stepped forward. "Adam—"

He rubbed a hand over his hair, taking Eleanor's hand with a long exhale. "Forgive me. I am simply… overwhelmed. There is no need to discuss the Beaumonts and my… rather strong opinions of them." He gave a strained smile. "I am happy to have you home. We have many items of greater importance to discuss.

I will have a room prepared for you immediately and make a place in the nursery for Arthur. Ella will be happy to have a new friend."

"I'll take the orders to the maid," Margaret piped in from her place near the door. She hobbled out into the hallway, and Eleanor could hear her loud, boisterous requests echoing through the halls.

"Are you certain you have room for Arthur and me?" She had not known that Adam had a family, and another guest staying. The house was not large, and she hated to be a burden. But she had nowhere else to go.

"Yes, of course. You are always welcome here." Adam gestured for Eleanor to sit. He and Amelia took a seat in two chairs across from her. Ella sat on Amelia's lap, and Arthur sat on Eleanor's.

Adam took a deep breath, his eyes fixed on Eleanor's face. She had forgotten how much he looked like their father. It filled her with a pang of sorrow. "I will begin with the first, and most pressing question I have," Adam said. "Where have you been these last five years?"

Although her brother's voice was gentle, it still struck her hard. Why was it so difficult to be honest with her own family? She had grown so accustomed to lying. Pretending she loved Mr. Quinton to avoid his punishments and anger. Pretending to be happy and comfortable in her home and in the company of her few neighbors. "I have been in Northumberland, and that is the truth."

Adam sat back, exchanging a look with Amelia. "That is something we guessed but could not justify spending the money it would require to go there in search of you. We very well could have been wrong. We could find no trace of Mr. Quinton's location. He abandoned the regiment and none of his friends knew where he went."

Eleanor blinked. "You did not believe the words in my letter?"

"At first we did, but the more I pondered over it, nothing seemed to make sense. Your abrupt departure did not align with your character."

Amelia peeked around her daughter's shoulder. "I had not yet had the privilege of meeting you, so all I learned of your character was through Adam's words. I did not believe any woman of sense would leave the side of her dying father, especially when the man she intended to elope with was a man her father did not approve of. That is what ultimately led me to suspect something was amiss."

Something was indeed amiss, then and now. Eleanor wrung her hands together. "Thank you for searching for me. I—I didn't know I was so greatly missed."

Adam looked equal parts joyous and angry. "I missed you more than you know. Please tell me everything Eleanor. You know you can trust me."

She gathered her strength, deciding the best course of action would be to tell Adam and Amelia of her plight, from the very beginning up until the day she fled. There was one detail she had banished from her mind, one that she could never tell speak aloud if she hoped to keep Arthur safe.

"I loved Mr. Quinton," she began, "or… I was quite certain that I did. He flattered me, he gave me gifts, kind words, generosity. He made me feel more important than I had ever felt in my life. I see now that it was all a trick. Through a member of his regiment, he learned of the dowry that was given to me through our uncle."

Adam sat up straighter. "You had a dowry?"

"No one knew of it besides Papa. He intended to keep it secret. Fifteen thousand pounds would draw in the greediest of men, Papa said. He advised me to keep it a secret, and I tried. But Mr. Quinton discovered it. I thought I could trust him."

Adam seemed to guess at the rest, his face hardening.

"We had planned to elope. I knew Papa did not approve of Mr. Quinton, but I still wished to marry him. I thought I loved him. I was certain that I could come visit often after our marriage. Before we could carry it out, I learned that Mr. Quinton was only interested in my dowry, and I was heartbroken. I declared that I would never marry him. But before I could escape, he forcibly took me to Gretna Green. He threatened to come back to Brighton and hurt you and Papa if I did not marry him. I did not know what to do." She shook her head, her stomach swimming with nausea at the memory. "We were married before the day was over." She tried to pause, but the words continued pouring out of her. "Through the last five years, he has gambled nearly all of my dowry away. When he died, Arthur and I finally had our opportunity to escape."

Adam's chest rose and fell with a heavy breath. Amelia's eyes shone with tears. She rushed forward to sit beside Eleanor on the sofa, touching her knee gently. "I am so sorry you were forced to endure such things. I cannot imagine the fear and loneliness you must have felt. You poor thing."

"If he were still alive, I might have killed him myself," Adam grumbled, coming to stand beside Eleanor as well. He sat against the edge of the sofa, taking her hand. "You are home now. You are safe. I should have tried harder to find you. I should not have given up."

"There is no way you could have known. Mr. Quinton fooled everyone."

"Not Papa." Adam's voice hardened. "Do you suppose Lord Ramsbury knew?"

Amelia met his eyes for a long moment before she shook her head. "When I saw him and his wife recently, I thought him to be a changed man. If he knew anything else, he would have confessed it to us by now. I am sure of it."

"I am not sure of it," Adam said. "I will go to his home tomorrow and ask him."

"That is not necessary," Amelia said, shaking her head.

Adam did not appear intent to drop the idea. He didn't speak of it further, but he seemed to tuck the idea away for later discussion. "Are you certain Mr. Quinton did not leave you a jointure?"

Eleanor sighed. "Yes."

"As I understand it, the common law would entitle you to one third of his properties at least, even without a premarital contract. But we will need to speak with a man more familiar with the law to affirm such details. I will take care of you and Arthur regardless of the result of such a discussion, but I do wish for you to reap all that you can in the way of money and property from such a miserable marriage. You deserve it."

Eleanor nodded, relief pouring through her at her brother's kindness. He would not turn her away. She had been foolish to think he would. But she still had not mentioned the issue that was the most pressing—the elder Mr. Quinton.

It was an irrational fear. He would not find her in Brighton. He would not have any way to prove what she had done, and he would not take Arthur from her. She repeated the reassurances to her heart over and over, until she started to believe them.

Chapter 4

There was something about a quiet house that led the mind to think of ridiculous scenarios. Henry Beaumont shook off the thought for what felt like the hundredth time. No, Mrs. Quinton had not been lying to him. What reason could she have to lie? He had mistaken her fearful expression and shifting eyes. Hadn't he?

Henry put his face in his hands as he sat at his dining room table. Growing up in a home with a father, mother, elder brother, elder sister, and younger sister, he was still not accustomed to the eerie silence of hearing just one fork scraping across a glass dish at dinner. His own.

He picked up his goblet and took a swig, trying, once again, not to think about the meal he had shared the day before with Mrs. Quinton and her coachman. He had been reflecting and dwelling on it for the last twenty-four hours instead of performing the duties of managing his estate that he ought to have been focusing on. Regardless of whether or not Mrs. Quinton was telling him the truth about all things, he knew that she had lied about at least one thing. Her husband was not alive and well and sending her and her son off on a trip to Brighton.

He was dead.

There were definite benefits to being the brother of one of the most influential peers in the county. His brother, Edward, never missed a piece of news or gossip, having connections to all circles of society, and being admired and respected by all. Edward had many friends that knew of Mr. Quinton's death and had been informed of it soon after it occurred.

It had occurred, Henry learned, just over one week ago. Edward had stopped by earlier that day on a ride with his wife, and upon Henry's mention of Mrs. Quinton's visit, Edward had broken the news.

Needless to say, Henry's confusion had then doubled.

He pushed away from the table, wiping his mouth with a napkin. It wasn't mere curiosity that made him eager to speak with Mrs. Quinton again. He wished to discover the truth because he worried over her. He had never seen such a fearful expression—such a permanent one—upon any face. He did not like it, and he knew that it certainly did not belong there. If there was any way he could help her and her son, he needed to find a way to do it.

The most effective way of finding the answers he sought, would be to go directly to the source. One might suspect the source to be Mrs. Quinton herself, but Henry knew that his brother was often the best source of information in all of Brighton. He had connections Henry could only dream of. The only connection Henry had was to Edward, which was a beneficial connection, indeed.

Henry set out for Brighton around two o'clock, arriving at Edward's home within the hour. He dismounted from his Arabian, knocking on the front door.

He found Edward in his study, sorting through his ledger. Edward glanced up, the blue of his eyes sparking with surprise. "Did you miss me already? Lud, brother, you need to find a wife." Edward gathered a stack of papers into his hands and rapped it against the table, straightening out the corners. A blonde curl fell over his forehead, adding to the devil-may-care appearance his brother flaunted. Though Henry shared the same blue eyes and blond hair, he was fairly certain his eyes had never sparked with mischief, and he preferred to keep his hair neat and as far from devilish as possible.

Edward had always teased Henry, saying that if he did not have any inheritance then he ought to become a vicar for his profession. There were times Henry wished for the life of a vicar, rather than the life of solitude he lived, managing his Worthing estate and the farms attached to it.

"I am still quite confused over my conversation with Mrs. Quinton," Henry said. "I hoped you could offer a bit of enlightenment," Henry said, pulling a chair closer to Edward's desk and sitting down.

"You have been treating me as much more intelligent than I truly am of late."

"You have become more intelligent since you married Grace. She has taught you well."

Edward chuckled. "See, once again, I affirm my point. You need to find a wife, and then you will not have to consult *me* with all your curiosities. You will find that a wife is a much better advisor than I will ever be."

Henry refrained from rolling his eyes. "I have given

you plenty of worthy advice in your life. I am not looking for advice from you. I thought you may have information that could help me. Mrs. Quinton lied about her husband being alive, and I cannot seem to stop wondering why."

"You always were a curious one, weren't you?" Edward laughed under his breath as he set down the stack of papers, leaning his elbows on the table to give Henry his full attention.

"I am worried for her. Returning to Brighton after her mysterious departure five years ago is going to hurt her reputation. I do not understand why she lied about her husband's death. What reason could she have for that?"

"Perhaps she knew she would never see you again and decided to spare herself a thorough questioning about the method of her husband's demise."

"I am not so insensitive as that."

"No, indeed. I am quite certain you are the most sensitive man of my acquaintance."

Henry smiled, unable to help it. "And you are the most intolerable."

"When my wife calls me intolerable, she means it as a compliment."

Henry chuckled. "Grace and I have never been more different."

Edward laughed before his expression grew slightly more serious. "Yes, I admit that when you told me of your conversation with Mrs. Quinton, I was quite curious myself. Her husband was a friend of mine, and I was surprised at the time to hear of his intentions of marrying Eleanor. He did not seem the sort of man to marry at all, unless it was for advantage. Eleanor did not have any dowry that I knew of, so I assumed it was for love. It was an elopement, as you know, and I was asked to keep it a secret until they could carry it out and move to London. I honored my friend's request, but I must admit the entire situation felt rather… strange. It was out of Mr. Quinton's character and as I understand it, out of Eleanor's character as well."

Henry tapped the oak desk with his fingertips. "Do you suppose Mr. Quinton was not the good man you thought he was? You did not see Mrs. Quinton that day. She did not appear to be on a joyful holiday. She appeared to be… fleeing. Running. Hiding. I cannot explain it. And then her son…he appeared afraid of everything and everyone. That does not simply happen to a child unless it is caused by something. What sort of a man was your friend Mr. Quinton?"

Edward shook his head slowly. "I am no longer certain." He rubbed his jaw, an idea hovering clearly on the surface of his expression.

"What is it?" Henry asked.

Edward sighed. "I doubt I will be welcome…but we could pay a visit to Adam Claridge's residence and seek our answers there. Or, we could simply keep our noses out of business that is not our own."

"It has become our business, Edward. You must take responsibility for the part you played with aiding Mr. Quinton in his secret elopement. And… I wish to help Mrs. Quinton in any way I can." Henry fixed his gaze on his brother, begging him with his eyes.

"If I could have half the heart and goodness that you have, Henry…" Edward shook his head, a slow smile pulling on his lips. "You simply cannot be swayed from the honorable, can you?"

"I'm afraid I cannot. But you—you were swayed from the dishonorable once."

"And I intend to never go back." Edward grinned. "So, I'm afraid that means I must help you."

"I'm afraid it does."

Edward stood, stretching his back and clasping Henry's hand in a firm shake. "Do you suppose the Claridges will receive visitors within the afternoon?"

"They may receive visitors, but I do not know if they will receive *you* as one of them."

Edward rubbed his forehead. "Adam does despise me. Amelia seems to have no quarrel with me. Perhaps she will convince him to receive our calling card with some measure of decorum. I will see if Grace wishes to accompany us. Amelia is sure to happily receive her."

They walked out to the hall, and Edward called for a servant to deliver their card to the Claridge residence, informing them of their pending arrival. Shortly after, they gathered their hats, Edward a beaver and Henry a top hat. Grace left their young son, Oliver, with the nanny and the three of them set off for the Claridge residence.

As they rode, Henry tried to plan what he would say. It was common practice to inquire after the safe arrival of Mrs. Quinton, her son, and their health after enduring such a wet storm on their journey. After that, he would simply see where the conversation led and what he could decipher from her words—whether she spoke truth or whether she continued with her lies.

The ride took less than twenty minutes by coach, and Henry led the way to the front door. They were let inside and directed to the parlor. The well-decorated room was filled with more company than Henry had expected. He was not well acquainted with the Claridges, but he clearly recognized Adam and his wife. An older woman sat beside them, a cane resting against her knee. The woman glanced up at Edward with a sour expression before standing and offering the customary bow of her head.

Edward nodded in return, greeting Adam and Amelia with nods in the same fashion. Henry greeted the party, pleased to see that the greetings he received in return were less sour than those Edward had received. They must have still believed him to be partially responsible for what happened to Mrs. Quinton—whatever that might have been.

Henry's eyes swept over the room again, and he found Mrs. Quinton and Arthur sitting in the far right corner, quiet and small, blending into the dark wallpaper behind them with their black hair. Henry offered a small smile to the little boy when he met his eyes, but the child glanced away quickly. Mrs. Quinton seemed to watch Henry's every step as he came farther into the room.

The room fell into silence for several seconds as they sat down. Adam's gaze was fixed firmly on Edward, and Henry had the distinct impression that the focus of this meeting would quickly come to be on Adam and Edward's quarrel. He hoped it could be resolved with enough time to discover more about Mrs. Quinton.

He glanced at her, meeting her eyes quickly before she darted them away. She stared at her hands in her lap.

"What has brought you here?" Adam asked, his deep voice breaking the silence.

Edward crossed his ankle over his knee. "It is my brother's errand that we are on. I am merely accompanying him." He turned to Henry.

Henry smiled, hoping to convey all his good intentions in one look. "Yes. As Mrs. Quinton may have told you, I met her and her son along their journey here. The weather was quite severe and—and I hoped to inquire after their health after being outside in such a storm." When he finished speaking, he turned to Mrs. Quinton in the corner.

She cleared her throat, the piercing blue of her eyes just as intense as her brother's, but without the malice. "We are quite well, Mr. Beaumont. I thank you for your concern. I give great credit to the hospitality you offered for the sustained health of myself and my son." She gave the slightest of smiles before her expression fell back into the fearful one he had seen the day before. It was as if she could give no other expression unless it was with great effort, such as the smile she had just forced onto her lips.

He studied her downcast eyes and shifting fingers. Was she nervous because she knew she had lied to him? Did she now realize he had caught her in the lie? He did not wish to add to her fear; he simply wanted to discover the reason behind it. He would have to be gentle about the way he brought it into the conversation. As he sorted through the options in his mind, he heard Edward's voice.

"I was very sorry to hear of your husband's death, Mrs. Quinton. Please accept my condolences."

Mrs. Quinton's complexion grew paler, her hands fidgeting faster over her skirts. Her son sat beside her, and she pulled him onto her lap, as if to hide behind him. Her eyes flicked to Henry's so quickly, he wondered if they had at all. She had been caught in her lie.

Henry shot Edward a berating glance, to which he simply winked, a motion so subtle that only the receiver would have noticed. He had clearly made Mrs. Quinton uncomfortable.

Edward's wife, Grace, sitting on Edward's other side, cast him a berating look of her own. Henry guessed that when Edward turned his head, he threw her a similar wink—or perhaps one with a bit more flirtation.

It took Henry a moment to take advantage of the door his brother had left open for him. He cleared his throat. "I did not know you were widowed, Mrs. Quinton."

The centers of her cheeks reddened, and he felt a pang of guilt for prying her secrets out of her. Secrets were often kept for a reason. "It was not something I wished to speak about." Her voice came out close to a whisper.

"I understand." Though Henry was far from understanding. "I am very sorry for your loss."

She nodded. Why was it that *she* did not appear sorry to have lost her husband?

Adam's voice cut through the air. "It has come to our attention that Mr. Quinton was not the sort of husband that my sister deserved. He was not a respectable man." He turned to Edward. "Is this something you were aware of, my lord, when you kept his abduction of my sister a secret?"

Henry watched as Edward's face blanched. He was not one to become easily uncollected. "Abduction?"

"Yes. She did not marry him willingly, and they were not living in London. He was keeping her in the North, prohibiting her to visit her family in Brighton."

Edward exchanged a glance with Henry. "I did not know of this, upon my word."

Adam eyed him with suspicion but remained silent. Awkwardness filled the air, pulsing with more vigor than Henry's heartbeat. Mrs. Quinton had been abducted? That would explain her constant fear. What had he been thinking coming here? It was obvious that he and Edward were not welcome. Especially Edward.

"Mrs. Quinton, was the rest of your journey—er—

comfortable?" Henry asked before he could think of a better question to break the silence.

"It was quite comfortable." She blinked, as if shocked at his level of stupidity for repeating himself.

"The weather was satisfactory?"

"Yes, it was."

Henry heard a choked sound come from beside him, knowing it to be Edward's laugh, suppressed behind his tight-lipped smile. Henry lacked the social charm in conversing that his brother had perfected, and it was never more obvious than in a moment like this.

"Forgive us for calling upon you at such a time," Henry said. "I presume you are eager to continue speaking with your family. Alone. If you need anything at all, I am happy to help you. I will help you in any way I can."

Grace had been engaged in a quiet conversation with Amelia, one that Henry had not noticed until Grace cleared her throat loudly, calling both Edward's and Henry's attention. "We mustn't leave yet," she said.

"Yes, please stay," Amelia said. She turned to Adam, placing her hand on his knee. "Grace has just informed me of a connection she has with Mr. William Harrison, her brother-in-law, a respected barrister living here in Brighton."

Adam's expression lightened for a moment.

"She is certain he will be able to assist us in the intricacies of Eleanor's financial dealings as well as her continued custody of Arthur."

Adam nodded slowly. "I would love to speak with Mr. Harrison."

"I will ensure he calls upon you this week," Grace said, smiling brightly. Her dark eyes mirrored the enthusiasm in Amelia's, each woman trying to alleviate the tension between their husbands.

Henry's eyes wandered over to Eleanor and Arthur, secluded in the corner. Why did she do that? Would she not wish to be near her family after being apart from them for so long? She still appeared nervous, as if she were hiding even from them. He could not explain the draw he felt to her. He shook the feeling from his shoulders, returning his attention to the conversation beside him.

The group arranged to have a meeting with Mr. Harrison at the earliest convenience for the barrister, and he and Edward and Grace were soon on their way.

Henry's brother turned to him as they stepped out the front door, waiting for the butler to close it behind them before speaking. "You might have made a greater effort to make our visit more awkward."

"Forgive me, but I could not think clearly amid the clear contention between Adam and yourself." Henry took a deep breath, rubbing one side of his face. "There is no sense in holding ill feelings toward another person. It will do nothing but hurt you."

"I always knew you should have been a vicar," Edward mumbled, earning a well-timed jab from his wife's elbow.

"There is always something to be learned from Henry," Grace said, her dark eyes inquisitive as they glanced across her husband, settling on Henry's face. "I have always wondered how the two of you were born of the same parents. You are as opposite as two brothers could be, at least in the way of character."

"We have been mistaken as twin brothers before," Henry said.

Grace laughed softly. "Yes, but I'm certain the very moment someone acquaints themselves with your distinct personalities, they would immediately contradict themselves."

"Do you mean to say that I am not saintly enough to be a vicar?" Edward asked, mock offense gleaming in his eyes.

Grace refused to answer, bursting into laughter.

Henry smiled at the ground as they crossed over the neat lawn and returned to the carriage. But his smile quickly faded when he remembered Mrs. Quinton and her fearful expression. There was something wrong with the entire situation, and he would not rest until he discovered how he could aid in mending it. For the first time since he had moved to Worthing, he felt he had a purpose.

Chapter 5

The very moment she heard the front door click shut, Eleanor released a long breath, her shoulders relaxing. Why must Mr. Beaumont look at her in that way? She had never felt so scrutinized in her entire life. Yet she could not blame him for it. She had lied to him about her husband's death, and he knew it.

She had spoken without thinking—she hadn't thought she would ever see Mr. Beaumont again, at least not until after she had established herself in Brighton and secured her safety from the elder Mr. Quinton.

The entire time—the very short time—that Mr. Beaumont and Lord and Lady Coventry had been there, she had felt vastly uncomfortable. Even now that they were gone, Adam and Amelia watched her with growing concern.

Adam tipped his head to one side, studying her with intensity. "Why did you tell Mr. Beaumont that your husband was still alive?"

"I did not wish to speak of it with a near stranger."

Adam nodded. He seemed intent to refrain from pressing her with more questions. She could see a battle in his eyes, even from her place across the room. His curiosity won out. "Did you ever say... how Mr. Quinton died?"

Her muscles clenched. "I did not." She licked her lips. "It was unexpected. I—I returned home one day and found him dead. I do not know what happened. That was when I fled with Arthur."

Adam glanced at his wife, who sat a little closer to the edge of her seat. "Have you not worked with a solicitor to settle the estate?"

"I did not have the time."

"Why not? With your husband dead, what reason could you have had to flee so quickly?"

She felt the familiar sensation of fear creeping over her skin and scratching icy fingers over her shoulder blades. "His father. He lived nearby. He was rather obsessed with his grandson—with Arthur—and often insisted on teaching him, taking him on trips to town. I do not trust him, so I often avoided it, but I could not always. I'm afraid... that he may be intent to find us again. I was afraid he would take Arthur if we did not leave quickly." Eleanor blinked, resisting the burning in her eyes. "I am certain he will find us. I do not know when, but I know he will. He knew the address of this home. I do not know what to do." She held Arthur's hand, keeping her voice low.

Amelia's brows had fallen, her face sullen. "Aunt Margaret, will you please take little Arthur and Ella to the nursery to play?" She glanced at Eleanor. "If you approve."

Eleanor nodded, setting Arthur on the floor. He glanced back at her, his eyes flashing with uncertainty as Margaret took his hand. "Go on. I will see you very soon."

Arthur followed quietly as Margaret and Ella left the room.

Adam rubbed his jaw, unrest evident in his features. "I am not familiar enough with law to say for certain, but your husband's father should not be permitted custody of the child."

"*Certainty* is what I'm desperately lacking at the moment."

"Our meeting with the barrister should be able to provide it." Adam stood, placing his hands on his hips. "But what you need now is a distraction. We shall find solutions to your problems then. For now, you are going into town with Amelia."

Eleanor's gaze drifted to the window. She could barely glimpse the sea from their angle, with its gently pulsing waves and pebbled shore, but that was where she wanted to go. She had only seen the unsettled, grey sea of the North for so many years. She wanted her Brighton sea again.

"May we take a walk by the sea too?" she asked, her voice little more than a whisper.

"Yes, of course," Amelia said. "We may do anything you wish."

Eleanor remembered that Arthur was up in the nursery. She hated leaving him for any measure of time. Amelia seemed to guess the reason behind Eleanor's hesitation, for she touched the sleeve of her ivory gown gently. "Not to worry. My aunt will take care of your son while we are away. Adam will be there too. Arthur will hardly notice the passage of time with Margaret telling him stories."

Eleanor did not doubt it. Arthur was quite comfortable with other women than herself, but she worried over his comfort in Adam's company without her nearby.

"We will not be away for long?"

"Only as long as you wish."

Eleanor was not accustomed to having things her way. The notion felt entirely new and strange. After fetching her bonnet and gloves, she and Amelia set out for the seaside. As they walked, she tipped her head back slightly, letting the rare sunlight kiss her cheeks. The warmth spread through her entire body, filling her with confidence in the future. Yes, perhaps the elder Mr. Quinton would find her and Arthur in Brighton. But at least they were no longer alone, and that was something to take great comfort in.

A card arrived the next day from Grace, inviting Eleanor, and whoever she wished to accompany her, to her estate, where the barrister would be waiting to discuss any questions they might have.

The timing came quite fortuitously, for Eleanor also received a letter that morning. Extended to her on a salver, she had felt the foreboding slipping through the wax seal and thick foolscap before she had even read a word. It was addressed to Mrs. William Quinton.

You might imagine my surprise and grief when I entered my son's home to find him dead. Even greater than that was my surprise to find you and my grandson gone. I expect this letter has reached you, for I know of no other place you might have run than to your childhood home in Brighton. As I have reflected upon why you might have fled and why you might have left your husband dead, I have come to a conclusion that I cannot deny. You were involved in his death somehow, and now you hope to escape the consequences.

It is my intention to ensure you do not escape them. The

first consequence I will relay to you is that you will surrender your custody of your son to me. Should you choose to evade this request, I will not rest until I find the proof needed to convict you of involvement in my son's death. I offer you an opportunity to give me my grandson without any further punishment to yourself. The courts will be on my side given your fallen reputation and lack of connections. If you choose not to take this offer, and I successfully have you convicted, then you will be forced to surrender Arthur to me.

Should I receive no reply to this letter, I will come to Brighton myself to ensure you have received it and to collect my grandson. You have never been a worthy guardian to him, and I will not have him living under the care of a murderess.

I await your prompt reply.

Sincerely,

Mr. Quinton

Eleanor set the letter down on the dining table, her hands shaking. Adam had been watching her carefully as she read. Without a word, she passed the letter to him. Her heart hammered, and she quickly turned to Arthur, slicing his ham into smaller pieces as she tried to calm her racing pulse. What would Adam think of the accusations against her?

"What's wrong, Mama?" Arthur asked around a mouthful.

"Nothing is wrong." She gave a quaking smile, turning her gaze back to Adam as he read over the page. When he finished, he set the paper down with disgust, sitting forward in his chair. Amelia snatched the paper up from the table, her eyes skimming quickly over the words.

"Do you think Mr. Harrison will be able to help me?" Eleanor asked.

"Yes." Adam's voice was strained. "There must be a way to evade these demands."

Eleanor's plate had begun to look very unappetizing. She glanced at the clock, clinging to the hope that Mr. Harrison could indeed give her an opportunity to escape Mr. Quinton's influence. She closed her eyes against the surge of nausea that rose in her stomach. She should have known her swift departure would raise suspicion over the circumstances of her husband's death. She did not mourn her husband. Not in the slightest. But the relief she had found in his death was now quickly unraveling. His father was an even greater threat if he had the power to take Arthur from her, the one good thing that had come from those years of dread and heartache.

She looked at Adam, dreading the question she knew was coming.

"Eleanor—" Adam began. "Is there any truth to his suspicions?"

She felt her breathing increase in rate, but she stopped it before it could be noticed. "No."

"You do not know what happened to your husband?"

What was she doing? Why was she lying to her brother? It was as if she was physically prevented from trusting anyone, even her own family. As troubling as it was, she could not convince herself to defy the feeling. "No. I understand how it appeared, but I was not involved in his death."

Adam stared at her for a long moment before glancing away. "We must find a way to disprove it then."

Thankfully, less than an hour later, it was time to leave for their meeting with Mr. Harrison. Eleanor left Arthur with Margaret and Ella again, who went to the nursery with little hesitation. Arthur had begun speaking more in the last two days than Eleanor had ever heard him speak, prattling on with Ella about all the things he saw and heard, asking her questions that she had little answer to. Eleanor loved to see him at ease in such an unfamiliar place.

They took the trip to the home of Lord Coventry by coach. The moment they entered the library, a hush fell over the hurried whispers she had heard from the hall. The room was filled with more guests than she had expected, and she felt suddenly self-conscious under so many gazes.

The man who she assumed was Mr. Harrison sat behind an oak desk, a large book sitting in front of him. He smiled warmly, the expression giving her a moment of reassurance. Lord and Lady Coventry sat nearby.

So did Mr. Beaumont.

Eleanor's eyes settled on him last. He smiled softly. Warmth and comfort spread through her chest, the feeling influenced entirely by a mere smile. Eleanor let her gaze linger on his face for a moment, taking in every drop of confidence she could reap from it.

She sat down on the couch across from Mr. Harrison, and Adam and Amelia joined her.

After Lord Coventry introduced her to the barrister, she withdrew the letter for him to study. The entire room fell silent as Mr. Harrison's eyes took in the threatening message. His eyebrows rose as he finished, setting the letter down carefully on the table. His green eyes rose to meet hers. "I will assume that his accusations against you are false. Does he hold any influence in society?"

Eleanor shook her head. "He is a tradesman. He does greatly desire Arthur, as he has always thought me unworthy to care for his grandson. He is also living below the means he aspires to. My dowry supplied much of my husband's gambling funds, but he also used it to buy alternative properties. I'm afraid none of it belongs to me any longer."

"As of now, one-third of those properties belong to you, and the rest will be Arthur's when he comes of age. Considering that Arthur is the heir, whoever is in custody of him would have control over those properties. I do not know this Mr. Quinton, but I suspect he is not an honorable sort of man, one that would simply desire to be a guardian for his grandson because of a great attachment to him. Unless, of course, such an attachment was born of the grandson's inherent wealth."

Eleanor knew without a doubt that her father-in-law was less than honorable. "Yes, I believe that theory is very plausible." Her voice came out quiet.

Adam touched the edge of the desk, drawing Mr. Harrison's attention. "What might be done to stop him? Eleanor was not involved in any sort of crime, so he cannot prove it. Does his threat hold any validity?"

"I'm afraid it does." Mr. Harrison shifted uncomfortably. "Taking Mrs. Quinton's reputation into account, she will have a very difficult time swaying the courts to consider her as a better guardian than Mr. Quinton. There is much he could do to give them reason to doubt her ability to properly care for him. With no monetary jointure, Mrs. Quinton will be seen as destitute. There is also the matter of her elopement, and when accusations are raised over a matter of crime, her reputation will only suffer further, whether or not the crime can be proven."

Eleanor willed herself to remain calm, although unease had begun pounding against her chest. "Is there nothing we can do?"

Mr. Harrison rubbed his forehead, sharing a glance with Lord and Lady Coventry. Mr. Beaumont sat quietly, his brows contracted as he listened.

"Perhaps my influence might be used to aid her case," Lord Coventry said.

Eleanor felt Adam stiffen beside her, his annoyance clear before she even looked at him. "That will not be necessary."

"Why not?" Lord Coventry said. "As a peer of the realm I have a much greater influence in court than a tradesman, believe me. I will defend her reputation if it is challenged."

Mr. Harrison spoke before Adam could reply. "Yes, that would be helpful, but I'm afraid it may not be effective enough. You have no notable connection with Mrs. Quinton, other than a short acquaintance." He took a deep breath, turning his gaze back to Eleanor. "I know this is likely the last thing you would like to hear, but I think it is your most advantageous option. It is imperative that you marry again."

Her stomach lurched.

"A married woman has a much greater influence and a much greater chance at thwarting accusations such as those Mr. Quinton is intent on giving. I am certain if you marry, and especially marry a man that will connect you to the House of Lords, you will be able to keep your son indefinitely, as well as the land you are entitled to. Yes, you must marry, and you must do so quickly. Ideally before Mr. Quinton decides to take his trip to Brighton."

Dread poured over her, sending a heavy stone to settle in the pit of her stomach. She balled her hands into fists, intense fear threading its way into her heart. No. She could never marry again. She had forbidden it of herself—she had vowed to never trust a man again. How could she? She had been betrayed by the man she thought she loved. Panic set in fully, sending her heart into a crescendo.

"I cannot marry," she whispered. "There must be an alternative solution."

Mr. Harrison sighed. "I wish there was. I truly believe this to be the best way to keep both you and your son safe."

Adam had been silently listening. "It will be difficult," he said. "As you have noted, Eleanor's reputation has suffered greatly. I do not see how this will be carried out in the time it is needed. If a man is found that is willing to marry her, I will insist that I come to know the man's character thoroughly before allowing him to marry my sister. I will not have her endure the same heartache she already has. He will need to come with many endorsements."

Eleanor wrung her hands together. How could she leave the protection of her brother when she had just found her way home again? Where could she find a husband so quickly?

Lord Coventry nodded his agreement. "I know of several unattached men in the surrounding area. The Baron of Crawley comes to mind, but of course, it would take a great deal of sacrifice to marry without equal connections and wealth to offer. There are several other gentlemen of my acquaintance we might introduce to Mrs. Quinton. They may find other qualities in her to be enough to elicit a marriage."

"Have you considered Lord Keswick?" Grace asked. "He or his younger brother would offer the needed connections. They both have lovely properties in Sussex that would keep Eleanor and her son hidden and safe from Mr. Quinton."

Lord Coventry shook his head. "The eldest is recently married and the younger is quite determined to marry an heiress."

The barrister drummed his fingers on the table. "It will be difficult, to be sure." The optimism had begun to fade from the man's normally cheerful voice.

Eleanor felt a mixture of both relief and disappointment. She would likely not find a man to marry. But how could she risk losing Arthur? There was nothing she would not do to keep him, even if it meant risking a loveless marriage all over again. Her heart pounded as the room fell silent. Every voice had offered suggestions that were quickly rejected.

Or rather—all but one voice.

Mr. Beaumont had remained rather silent, his arms crossed and his blue eyes far more ponderous than Eleanor had ever seen them.

As the silence thrummed louder, Mr. Beaumont sat forward in his chair. "I will marry her."

Chapter 6

It took a moment for Eleanor to register the deep baritone voice that had just spoken a most unexpected phrase.

Everyone in the room fell even more silent than they had already been, which Eleanor had previously thought to be impossible. Every eye shifted to Mr. Beaumont.

His face mirrored the surprise she felt, as if he hadn't entirely intended to volunteer his *services*. Marry her? Eleanor had always believed there were limits to kindness, even among the most valiant of people.

She stared at him, trying to appear less shocked than she felt. Waiting for someone to speak felt like it lasted an eternity, but finally Mr. Beaumont broke eye contact, addressing the barrister. "My connections are not as great as a peer, but I happen to be the brother of one of the most influential peers in the county. By marrying me, Mrs. Quinton would be connected to Lord and Lady Coventry through far more than a mere acquaintance." Mr. Beaumont's tone was even and casual, offering the marriage as one might offer a spare egg to a neighbor. Did he not have higher aspirations for his life than to marry a widowed woman with a young child, one whose reputation would likely hurt his own? His conversation with her coachman came to mind, when he had said that he hoped only to marry for ardent love and affection. Why was he willing to sacrifice that now? Eleanor could hardly believe what she was hearing.

"Please, Mr. Beaumont," she said, her voice quick. "You have already helped me in so many ways." She had yet to thank him privately for paying her coachman. "There is no need to be so benevolent."

The barrister seemed to still be pondering the idea. His expression slowly lifted into a smile and he gave a nod. "I would not be so swift to deny Mr. Beaumont's offer, Mrs. Quinton. He makes a very valid point."

Eleanor could not deny that marrying Mr. Beaumont would be a much more desirable option than marrying a complete stranger. She had already seen Mr. Beaumont demonstrate a considerable amount of kindness, and if that was not a testament to a person's character, then she did not know what else could hold a greater weight. But she could not allow him to marry her strictly out of the goodness of his character. Could she?

She studied his expression, hoping to find a hint of selfishness there. His eyes were both calm and tempest tossed, as if he himself were conflicted over what he had just offered.

"Mrs. Quinton," he began. "I told you I would help you in any way I could. I am a man of my word. If a marriage between us will protect you and your son, I would be honored to help you."

Eleanor turned to Adam, seeking reassurance from him. His expression was difficult to read from his profile, but she could see that his jaw was set firmly, and that could only mean one thing. "No," he said. "We will find a different family to connect Eleanor with. Surely there is another option."

Amelia gave an exasperated sigh at the same moment Grace did, although Amelia's was slightly louder. "Adam, I'm afraid the decision is not yours to make."

"I am acting as Eleanor's guardian."

Eleanor had known Adam to be very protective of her for her entire life, but she had never seen him so protective as she had since returning to Brighton. She could not blame him for it, and she was grateful, but she had learned in her time away that she needed to make her own decisions, no matter how difficult.

She lowered her voice to a whisper. She hoped Mr. Beaumont could not hear it from across the room. "Adam—I do believe it is the best option I have, and a very good one. Mr. Beaumont has shown himself to be honorable in every way." She hoped it were true.

Adam drew a deep breath. "Are you certain?"

"Yes."

"Very well." Adam still appeared displeased with the arrangement, but her assuredness seemed to have calmed him.

Mr. Harrison watched them carefully from across the desk, his gaze flickering to Mr. Beaumont and back again. "As I said before, this is very advisable. I can think of no better option for the safety of both Mrs. Quinton and the child. And I can speak my own endorsement of Mr.

Beaumont's character. He is a good man. So. Will you marry him?"

Eleanor's eyes locked with Mr. Beaumont's again, and she found within them enough strength to answer. "I will."

Mr. Beaumont's face showed little emotion but the residual shock from his offer. She felt a pang of guilt stab through her chest. Did he regret it already? She glanced at Lord Coventry, who now leaned his head on his hand. There was a feathery smile on his lips, mingled with a look of disbelief. "I can procure a special license for the marriage if that is desirable," he said, looking up. "It would be wise to keep it as secret as we are able."

"How soon could you procure one?" Mr. Harrison asked.

"As soon as next week. Will that give you both enough time to make any needed arrangements?"

Eleanor's stomach flipped. She had hoped to stay home for much longer than one week, to enjoy Brighton a bit longer before being torn away from it again. She stopped herself. She was not being *torn* away this time. She was going willingly to protect Arthur. Mr. Quinton would not be able to find her easily in Worthing, and he wouldn't be able to take Arthur. She felt a new surge of courage at that thought.

Eleanor nodded. "I will do whatever is needed." She tried not to look at Mr. Beaumont again, but she couldn't help her own curiosity.

"One week will be just fine," he said.

"Where will the ceremony be held?" Mr. Harrison asked. "I will speak with the vicar and arrange his services for the chosen date and time."

"Wednesday next?" Adam suggested.

Mr. Beaumont gave a nod. "That will do just fine."

"We can hold it here in our drawing room," Grace said.

"That would be wise," Lord Coventry said. "The church bells declaring the marriage of a missing woman would draw a great deal of gossip." His voice carried a hint of humor. Eleanor could find nothing humorous about her current situation.

"Very well. It is settled, then." Mr. Beaumont stood, sharing a quick glance with Eleanor before walking toward her. "Will ten o'clock on Wednesday be a suitable time?"

She nodded, unsettled by his sudden approach. "Yes." The awkwardness was excruciating. Was she supposed to thank him? She thought that was probably the appropriate response, considering that he had offered to marry her solely to protect her and her son. She searched again for a sign of selfish motivation in his eyes, but she could find none. He did not desire her money, for she had none. He didn't desire her—she was no great beauty. He simply desired to give what he could to improve her life. Her mind raced with the oddity of such behavior. The unfamiliarity of it.

Before she could collect her thoughts and stammer her gratitude, the barrister recalled Mr. Beaumont's attention. "Are you certain you wish to carry this out?"

Eleanor froze. This was his opportunity to change his mind. Part of her wished he would. Then she would not feel so guilty.

"Yes."

Mr. Harrison's expression, still slightly grim, lightened. "Very well." He turned to Eleanor. "Please keep me informed of any other correspondence you receive from Mr. Quinton. I do not think he will be of any threat to your son now that you are to be married to Mr. Beaumont, but I am here to help you if needed."

"Thank you." *Thank you* was not such a difficult thing to say. Why had she been unable to say it to Mr. Beaumont? He must have thought her a simpleton or a very disagreeable person, neither of which he deserved to have to marry.

"I hope you will find much happiness together," Mr. Harrison said, his gaze shifting between Eleanor and her new betrothed.

The awkwardness only grew in weight, and Eleanor felt stifled by the entire room—the drawn curtains, the extravagant number of surrounding books, and all the eyes that rested on her. "Thank you." It was now *all* she seemed able to say.

She made to stand, and Mr. Beaumont stepped forward, offering his hand to help her up from the deep cushions. She hesitated much longer than she should have but took it firmly. Good heavens, her hand was so much smaller than his. He pulled her to her feet, releasing her hand the moment she was up. She avoided his eyes, feeling strangely shy.

Adam stepped up beside her, shaking Mr. Beaumont's hand. "Thank you for helping my sister in such a way. I am sorry to have doubted you." Eleanor watched as he and Lord Coventry exchanged a glance and was surprised to see Adam approach him.

"I'm glad to see that you are trying to atone for your previous mistakes." There was an edge of lightness to Adam's voice.

Lord Coventry raised his eyebrows. "Do you suppose we can be friends?"

"I think we can call it a truce for now."

Eleanor hated to have been the cause of any dispute but was glad to hear Adam's smile and a tone of apology in his voice.

"I must admit I didn't believe the claims that you were a changed man," Adam said. "I can see now that I was wrong. Your actions have shown it more than words ever could, and they will continue to show it as you use your connections in society for good."

"As I always have." Lord Coventry said.

Half the room chuckled at that, alleviating a small portion of the awkwardness.

Mr. Beaumont still stood near Eleanor, close enough that she could smell clean soap and fresh linen of his clothing. She clasped her hands together, staring down at them as if they were far more interesting than the conversation taking place around her.

"I will do all I can to ensure you and Arthur are comfortable and happy," Mr Beaumont said. His words struck her, deep and jarring.

Her eyes found his, and she was shocked to see the sincerity in them. "Why?"

He seemed taken aback by her question, but she couldn't help but ask it. Her own husband had not cared for her happiness before, and now a near stranger cared deeply enough for it to sacrifice his own chance at happiness—at true love, for her safety.

His features settled into a look of compassion. "You deserve it."

Did she deserve it? She had lied more times to count in the recent days.

"As do you." She glanced up at him, realizing how tall he was beside her. The top of her head must have only reached to the level of his mouth. Her late husband had been the same height as her, leaving his eyes level with hers. Oh, how she had hated those eyes.

She searched for something to say, uncomfortable with the persisting silence. "You will be pleased to hear that my coachman never ceased to compliment your meal on our drive to Brighton."

Mr. Beaumont smiled. "I cannot say that I am surprised."

"He does have a quick tongue. I don't think he stopped talking at all."

His eyes glinted with mirth. "If one is going to speak so continuously, it should very well be flattering words. Especially if they are aimed toward me."

He seemed more like Lord Coventry than ever in that moment. His confidence was reassuring, and she knew the arrogance was a fabrication. Her shoulders relaxed as relief flooded her. As greatly as it terrified her to marry another man, if she was to be forced into it, then that man might as well be Mr. Beaumont. She could think of no better alternative. With her worries put to ease, she felt herself smiling a little. Optimism had become her friend over the last five years. She could not let it abandon her now.

"We will come together a week hence for the wedding," she heard Adam say.

She pulled her gaze from Mr. Beaumont's. Adam ushered her toward him where he stood near the door with Amelia. Eleanor joined them, thanking Mr. Harrison before the trio departed. Why could she not find the words to thank Mr. Beaumont? She cursed herself silently as she entered the carriage and set off toward home.

The reality of what had just occurred seemed to strike her then, threading up her arms and finding solidarity with her heart. She would soon have a new home outside of Brighton. But as long as Arthur was safe, she could undertake any new challenge.

❦

"What the devil have you done?" Edward asked, his tone exasperated as the last of their guests exited the drawing room.

Henry could not look away from the door, his mind in a distant place. What *had* he done? The offer to marry Mrs. Quinton had simply slipped out of him, born from the look of fear and helplessness on the woman's face.

"I could not stand by, entirely capable of helping the matter, and do nothing." Henry's voice was resolute as he turned to face his brother and his uncharacteristically quiet wife.

"There is a line to be drawn when it comes to goodwill, Henry." Edward rubbed a hand over his hair. "There was a time that I intended to sacrifice love in a marriage for the sake of keeping my inheritance, which was the only thing important to me at the time. Only later did I realize that Grace was all that truly mattered. Love was all that mattered."

Henry had always hoped to marry a woman that he loved deeply, but he had felt compelled to abandon all reason at the chance to help Eleanor. "The only thing important to *Eleanor* is her son's safety," Henry said. "I will sacrifice that which is important to me if it means preserving that which is important to her. I daresay a child's happiness and well-being are far more important than my ambitions of finding love."

Edward stared at Henry for a long moment, his features relaxing. "I have never fully understood your inborn selflessness. You ought to try to be a bit more selfish. You make the rest of humanity look quite evil in comparison."

Henry lowered his gaze, embarrassed by the rare praise from his brother. "It is no great sacrifice. At any rate, I am lonely at my Worthing estate. The company will be refreshing."

"Ah. There is one selfish motivation. Are there any others?"

Henry refused to admit the draw he felt to Eleanor. He wanted to come to know her, to make her smile, to give her some reason to find joy after she had endured so much heartache. He found her intriguing in a way he could not explain. No, his motivations were not entirely selfless. He did not wish to see her wed to another man, one that would not care for her and her child the way he would try his hardest to do. He wanted to protect her, to see her well. To ensure she found the happiness she deserved.

Edward took a deep breath. "I suppose I am just disappointed. Now you have no chance at finding a woman to marry that you truly love."

Grace placed a hand on Edward's arm, shaking her head. "No, that is not true at all. This entire situation could become the perfect beginning to Henry's love story."

Edward gave her a skeptical look. "You cannot believe Henry loves Eleanor."

"Not yet, but I would not condemn the idea. You certainly did not love me when we first met." Her brown eyes took on a teasing glint, pulling a smile from Edward's face. He kissed the top of her head as he laughed. "And you certainly did not love me. Not even remotely."

"I hated you," she said without a flinch or hint of apology. "And you deserved it."

Edward opened his mouth in protest, but she continued, covering his lips with her fingertips.

"However, I grew to love you more than I ever thought possible. Henry and Eleanor are already well on their way. I see no signs of hatred between them. I'm certain they will learn to love one another if they choose to."

Henry had been watching the exchange with growing unease. "Choose to?"

Grace turned to face him, a thoughtful expression marking her features. "Love is at least half choice, just like happiness is. If you choose to have it, you are already halfway there. The rest will present itself when you least expect it."

Edward, ever the romantic, rolled his eyes, pulling his wife closer. "I will not pretend to understand your philosophies on love, but if they took any part in bringing you to me, then I will adore them always."

Grace smiled, leaning her head against his shoulder. "You are quite fortunate that I love you. If not, I would have throttled you at least a dozen times already."

Edward laughed.

Henry drew a deep breath, hoping the sound would call his brother and sister-in-law's attention back to the matter at hand. He knew he could not undo his decision to marry Mrs. Quinton, but he needed help understanding how to move forward. His decision had been entirely spontaneous, and he did not deal well with spontaneity.

Edward's eyes settled on Henry again, the heaviness returning to them. "Do you realize the level of scrutiny you will be under? Society will wonder why you have rushed into such a marriage with a recent widow, one whose reputation is already far from intact."

"I realize that." Henry said, though his understanding had not entirely bloomed until that moment.

"Very well," Edward said with a sigh. "It seems we have a wedding to plan."

Chapter 7

Henry had always imagined his wedding day at the local church, with his friends and family flanking the road as his carriage drove off with his new wife, whom he would have deeply loved. The weather would have been warm and bright, without a single cloud to be seen.

He was fairly certain this day could not have been more opposite.

He and Eleanor were married by the local vicar in his brother's drawing room. After a simple signing of papers and a brief word, they were declared man and wife. They hardly made eye contact. The rain had started while they were inside, and he and Eleanor and her son had to make a run for the waiting carriage.

Henry had offered to carry Arthur, but Eleanor had been quite insistent against it. Henry also could have never predicted the presence of his wife's child at his wedding, one who was now his stepson. It was all so very strange.

When the footman closed the carriage door behind them, Henry wiped the droplets of rain and nervous perspiration from his brow. "Rain seems to follow you wherever you go, Mrs. Quinton. Er—Eleanor." He glanced at her for approval, embarrassed that he had called her by her previous surname. She was now his wife. He was allowed to use her Christian name now, wasn't he? She did not seem to be offended by it. They were married after all.

His head pounded. *Married?* The idea would take a great deal of time to sink in.

"And you always seem to be near me when it does rain." She offered the smallest of smiles, but she appeared as nervous as he felt.

"Fortunately, as you know, my estate is equipped with a warm hearth and a talented cook, one that I am told is the best in the county." His intention had been to pull another smile from her, but it seemed she was incapable of smiling larger than a tight-lipped, simple twitching of her mouth. What was happening inside that head of hers?

Arthur looked up at him from his place on the pink and white striped cushion beside her. His clear blue eyes were nearly identical to his mother's in color, and his hair was almost as black. Henry had hardly heard the boy utter a single word. He appeared old enough to speak but seemed too shy to do it. His mother seemed just as shy in that moment.

Growing up in the same home as Edward, Henry had always been more shy, more reserved, something of a shadow to his older brother. Henry could likely blame Eleanor's late husband for casting a shadow over Arthur. The boy seemed to observe everything around him as if it were to be regarded with suspicion. It seemed he learned the trait from his mother.

Eleanor stared intently out the carriage window, but watched Henry with quick glances, a wariness in her gaze.

"I hope you will both be comfortable in your new home," he said. "I hope to find many things to keep you both happy and entertained. How do you enjoy spending your days, Eleanor?"

She seemed surprised to have been asked such a question. She placed a hand against her collarbone. "Me?"

"Yes."

"Oh—well, I... I have not thought about that for a long while." She gave him a shaky smile, one he recognized to be entirely forced.

She had not thought about her favorite pastimes? "Do you enjoy music, painting, reading?"

She shifted. "Well... life was quite different in Northumberland. I stayed inside with Arthur most days, and...that is all, really. I told him stories to pass the time and sang songs as well. We did not have any instruments, very few books, and no supplies for sewing or stitching. There was little to do except be in one another's company." She cast her eyes downward, smoothing back her son's hair as he stared steadfastly at Henry, as if afraid to take his eyes away for a moment.

A pang of sympathy struck Henry squarely in the chest. "Did you venture outside often?"

"I'm afraid not. The weather was often too severe for Arthur at his young age, and we were not allowed—" Her voice trailed off. "We thought it best to stay indoors."

He found at least one explanation for her reserved countenance and porcelain white skin. "Do you like animals?"

Eleanor's eyes lifted. "We had a pet once."

Henry took note of that in his mind. He turned his gaze to the little boy. "Do you like animals, Arthur?"

Henry was fairly certain the boy would be terrified of anything that moved.

He sunk deeper into his cushion, glancing up at his mother before speaking in a soft, slightly raspy voice. "I wike tigers."

"Tigers?" Henry smiled, widening his eyes in an animated fashion.

Eleanor gave another of her tight smiles. "Of the few books we did have, one documented the life of a tiger."

"I see," Henry said, turning his attention back to Arthur. "I have something quite close to a tiger at my home. It is going to be your home too. Would you like to meet her when we arrive?" He had a neighbor with kittens, so that would have to pass for a young tiger.

Arthur's face grew even whiter, his eyes rounding. He shook his head. "I wike wooking at pictures of tigers. That's all."

"This is a nice tiger. A small one."

Arthur clung to his mother's arm, his chin beginning to quiver. "I don't want to see a tiger, Mama."

Henry raised his hands. "I was only jesting. It is not a tiger. It is a kitten."

Arthur kept his face buried in the sleeve of his mother's dress, a simple white muslin. Eleanor patted his arm, whispering reassurances in his ear while Henry took to staring out the window in silence.

Blast it all. He had managed to terrify his new stepson within minutes. He raked his fingers through his hair, exhaling heavily. He had quite the task before him.

***

After what felt like the passage of hours, the carriage finally arrived in Worthing, pulling up the drive of Henry's estate. Eleanor and Arthur did not have much in the way of possessions, so Henry noted that he would have to set aside funds for new clothing for them both.

The estate had many books that would enable Arthur to begin his education, but he had little in the house that would appeal to a female. What did women enjoy doing? Growing up, his mother could often be found in the drawing room with a piece of embroidery or knitting. His estate had many musical instruments that Eleanor could learn to play or practice on. Before her first marriage she must have enjoyed other pastimes. It was as if she had forgotten who she had once been.

He helped Eleanor down from the carriage. She touched his arm lightly before letting go. Before he could help Arthur down, she scooped him up.

Henry felt entirely helpless. What had he done to make the boy so afraid of him? All he had done was mention a tiger, something which the boy had claimed to like. He took a collective breath as he led the way across the grass to the front doors.

He had thought he might lead his wife by the hand, or even the arm after their wedding, at the very least, but Eleanor seemed quite intent to keep her arms crossed or hold tightly to her son, as if Henry might swipe him away. Did she not trust him at all? He felt as if two great pieces of glass were walking along beside him, capable of shattering at any moment. What had he gotten himself into?

"Mr. Cranford, how do you do?" Henry said as they walked through the door.

The butler took Henry's hat and gloves. "Quite well. The rooms have been prepared for your wife and stepson."

He gave a polite smile to Eleanor and Arthur. The housekeeper, Mrs. Simmons, stepped forward to take Eleanor's things. Henry had assigned the same maid, Mary, who had previously been a maid-of-all-work, to be Eleanor's lady's maid. She had been quite enthused over her new responsibilities, and Henry trusted her ability to make Eleanor both comfortable and fashionable.

"At your service, m'lady," Mary said. "Would you like to rest in your chambers?"

Henry had hoped to give Eleanor a tour of the home upon her arrival. He was glad to see her shake her head. "I feel well rested, thank you, although my son might like a nap." She glanced at Arthur, who gave a yawn in answer.

"I have not yet hired a nursemaid," Henry said.

Eleanor shook her head. "There will be no need for one."

Henry hesitated. He hoped Eleanor would venture outside, socialize with other women, enjoy the things she had been lacking in the recent years. If she was constantly with her son, she would not have such privileges. He knew the importance of being a present and caring mother, as his own mother had been very caring and kind, but he also knew the importance of caring for oneself. His mother had been overwhelmed by him and Edward many times, and he could not blame her.

"Are you certain? She would just be here to help with bathing and dressing Arthur in the morning and taking him to breakfast."

Eleanor seemed to consider it. "I suppose that will be fine."

"I will prepare an advertisement in town soon," he said. "I do have a bedroom for Arthur, directly beside your chambers." And his. Henry had moved his room to the adjoined chambers designed for the master and mistress

AN UNEXPECTED BRIDE

of the house. He hoped it would not frighten Eleanor to have him sleeping just beyond her door. It seemed that everything put her on edge.

Henry felt as though he were hosting two guests; the three were far from feeling like a family. He could only hope that in time they could. He remembered Grace's words about love, how it was a choice. He did not think Eleanor was even close to choosing to love him. The first thing he needed to focus on would be to ensure she did not *fear* him.

Henry was silent for too long, lost in thought. Eleanor began following Mary up the stairs, Arthur in tow.

"Would you like a tour of the house?" Henry asked, or rather—spurted.

She turned, her eyes round. "I—I suppose. Yes, I should acquaint myself with the property."

And your new husband. "Very well. When Arthur is settled for his nap, I will meet you here." Henry smiled.

Eleanor acknowledged his words with a small nod before walking up the stairs. He was thankful Mary was talkative. Perhaps she would teach Eleanor how to speak a little more. The moment they were out of sight, he exhaled, slumping against the banister. He could feel a headache coming on.

Mr. Cranford cleared his throat, but it sounded something like a chuckle. "I wish you all the best of luck, sir."

Luck. It would take much more than that.

⚜

"I hope you'll find this to your liking," Mary said, smoothing her palms over the quilts on Eleanor's bed. Arthur had begun exploring the room, babbling on about the smooth wood of the wardrobe and the soft velvet of the curtains. Away from the company of Mr. Beaumont, he had begun speaking again. "Mama! Wook! A bird!" He pointed a slim finger out the window where a robin had perched on the windowsill. "Is the tiger going to eat it?"

Eleanor smiled, coming to stand beside him. "No, there is no tiger here."

His little shoulders slumped in relief, and Eleanor was quite envious of the motion. She had felt no relief since learning of her required marriage. The entire day had been extremely nerve-wracking and awkward. She could not seem to gather her thoughts around Mr. Beaumont, much less her words.

"Let me show you to Arthur's room," Mary said, guiding them to the door. Arthur seemed quite comfortable around the maid already, having recognized her from their brief stay at the estate the week before. He seemed quite comfortable around everyone he met, except Mr. Beaumont. He was skeptical, and Eleanor fully understood why. It would take time for Arthur to grow comfortable with his stepfather.

Arthur's room was small, with a tiny wooden rocking horse in the corner near the window. Arthur stared at it, quite unaware of what a toy was. The only toys he had been given before had been ones that Eleanor made for him out of seashells and grass.

"Sit on it," she instructed.

Arthur stepped forward, swinging his leg over the wooden saddle. He placed his feet on either side, holding onto the wooden handles so tightly his fingers turned white. Eleanor pushed gently on the back, letting it rock. Arthur giggled.

"A precious boy, he is," Mary said. "I'll keep a close eye on him while you take your tour with your husband."

Her husband. It would take a long while before she was accustomed to hearing that. Her heart thudded as she walked out to the vast hallway. Her bedchamber was on the second floor, and she knew the house to have just two floors. She did not want her tour with Mr. Beaumont to take a long time. But how else would she become further acquainted with him? She had grown used to very limited communication with her late husband. She had avoided being close to him as much as possible, especially after Arthur was born. He had flattered her at first, apologized for forcing their marriage, claiming that he still loved her.

Mr. Beaumont seemed intent on communicating with her. He quite enjoyed asking her questions.

When she rounded the corner, she saw that he still stood at the base of the stairs. He greeted her with a smile. She held onto the banister, trying to appear unaffected as she descended the staircase.

"What did you think of your room?" he asked.

"It is very nice."

"If there are any improvements you would like to see made, do not hesitate to suggest them to me or Mrs. Simmons."

Eleanor thanked him with her eyes, as her tongue seemed quite intent to avoid functioning. Blast the man's blue eyes. Mr. Quinton had been charming too. He had appeared kind and caring. She had later discovered it all to be an act. What if Mr. Beaumont was only pretending too? How could she ever know for certain? She reminded herself that Mr. Beaumont had not told her any lies that she could detect. He had not fed her flattering words or false praise. That was a good start.

"We will begin with the main level, then the grounds."

Henry paused for a short moment before extending his arm. She took it, letting him guide her down the hall to the right. The halls were fairly bare, with few wall sconces and small tables. They walked until they reached a single door, and he opened it.

"This is my study. I spend much of my time here sorting through the financial records of the estate and other similar boring matters of business." He smiled, glancing at her face.

"I would not say it is boring," she said. "I often helped my father in his study. He gave me the responsibility of straightening his stacks of paper and securing them with clips." Her heart stung a bit at the memory. But it was a happy sting, the sort of hurt that had shaped her for the better, not the worse. Those were the memories she allowed herself to dwell on—the memories that had pushed her through the darkest days of her life.

"Do you miss him?" Mr. Beaumont asked.

She blinked up at him. "Yes. Very much."

"My father died four years ago."

"Do you miss him?" She felt strange repeating his question, but there was a certain indifference in his tone that made her curious.

Mr. Beaumont seemed to ponder over the question for a long moment. "Not as keenly as I am sure you miss your father. Mine did not give me very much to miss, I'm afraid. I rarely saw him." His eyes flashed with hurt, but it was so brief, she was unsure she had seen it at all.

He closed the door, leading her farther down the hall to the library. He pushed the doors open, revealing a room with a lofty ceiling, every wall lined with bookcases, each bookcase filled. A table and wooden chairs rested near the fireplace, with a large armchair near the window.

"I think this would be the perfect place to begin educating Arthur," Mr. Beaumont said. "I thought we might search for the children's books and arrange a shelf just for him. He will be old enough to learn to read soon."

Eleanor felt a flicker of hope as she watched the excitement on Mr. Beaumont's face. Did he truly care about Arthur's education?

"We might even hire a tutor to school him, one trained in educating young boys."

Eleanor couldn't hide her surprise. "Truly? You would do that?"

"Of course." A slight scowl had marked Mr. Beaumont's brow. "I am his guardian now. I will do everything I can to ensure he is raised as any boy ought to be, with every opportunity he deserves."

A surge of gratitude enveloped her. Mr. Quinton had never suggested that he would give Arthur a quality education. All Mr. Quinton had cared about were his games and his property. He had never claimed Arthur as his own or shown any interest in him, except to threaten and frighten him for misbehaving, for speaking even a word or making a sound. Eleanor, he had always viewed as his property.

Her troubled thoughts must have reflected on her face. Mr. Beaumont stared down at her with concern before he stopped walking, turning to fully face her. "I wish to make something clear to you," he said.

Her heart thumped. Did he have a set of strict rules too? She lifted her chin, staring straight into his eyes. "Yes?"

"Not only is Arthur under my protection, but you are too. I will do all in my power to ensure your safety and your happiness. You are safe here, Eleanor. I give you my word."

His voice was deep and filled with conviction, his eyes fixed on hers with sincerity. She clung to his words, hoping with all her heart that they were true. She clenched her teeth against the tears that threatened to overwhelm her. After years of being stoic, of keeping her tears inside in the face of mistreatment and sorrow, how was it that she could be moved to tears over a few kind and genuine words?

She blinked fast, hiding the moisture in her eyes. At least Arthur was not here to see it. "Thank you, Mr. Beaumont," she said, finally able to find those two very important words.

He smiled, and she felt threads of warmth making their way through her chest as he extended his arm again. "You may call me Henry if you wish."

Eleanor hesitated. It seemed very informal. But he was her husband. Her mother had always called her father by his Christian name. Despite her every effort, her cheeks warmed as she said it.

"Thank you, Henry."

Chapter 8

"This is the dining room," Henry said, sweeping his open palm through the air. Her tour was almost complete, and Eleanor found herself not wanting it to end.

Eleanor took in the ornate, long table, the paintings on the walls, the simple chandelier above, and the intricate rug beneath the table. The room seated ten. She hoped Henry would allow her to invite her family to dine with them on occasion. The room could easily accommodate Adam and Amelia as well as Lord and Lady Coventry, who Eleanor had come to like immensely.

"Shall we move to the upper floor?" Henry asked.

Eleanor nodded, following him out of the room and toward the staircase. The second floor consisted of mostly bedrooms, but there was also the portrait gallery and a music room.

"Do you play any instruments?" Henry asked as he opened the door.

"I do not." Eleanor wished she had learned to play the pianoforte in her youth, but she had been all too consumed with more frivolous activities. Still, when she thought about her life before her marriage to Mr. Quinton, she found there was much to miss. She had been so happy, energetic, and free. She and her friends had gone to the assembly rooms often, flirting, dancing, playing cards. She had enjoyed perusing the Brighton shops and wearing beautiful accessories. She had a basic education, but she was far from proficient in French or any other subject expected of young ladies. She wished she had better spent her time. If she had been smarter, perhaps she might have seen Mr. Quinton for who he was.

"It is never too late to learn." Henry smiled again, sending another wave of warmth through her cheeks. She cursed herself for being affected by a mere smile. She had allowed Mr. Quinton's smiles to steal her heart, but he had soon after trampled it underfoot. She would not risk that again. Henry had no intention of loving her. He had only married her because…

Well, she did not have the answer. Henry was her protector, perhaps he could even become her friend. But nothing more.

"I have always wanted to learn the harp," she said, staring at the tall, golden instrument. She smiled softly. "When I was a child, I thought playing the harp would make me feel like an angel."

Henry stared at her, delight crossing his features. "I suspect you would look rather angelic playing it as well."

Flattery. That had been Mr. Quinton's first weapon. She felt her smile disappear, and she crossed her arms over her stomach. "Only because my mother had a painting of an angel playing a harp. I always associated the instrument with angels."

"I see." Henry nodded, his own smile fading. He cleared his throat. "Well, I would gladly hire you an instructor if you wish."

She shook her head. "That is all right. I will have little time to practice with Arthur running about."

"I will take him whenever you need time to yourself."

Eleanor's muscles twitched with alarm. "Take him?"

Henry's brow flattened. "Take him under my care. Look after him. The nursemaid will be able to help too."

She felt thoroughly stupid for needing such an explanation. Her nerves were on edge and had been for a very long time. "Yes, of course. That would be wonderful."

Awkwardness filled the air again, and she turned away, walking closer to the harp. She ran her finger along the golden neck, lightly plucking the strings. She observed the other instruments in silence, feeling the smooth wood of the cello beside it, and studying the chipped keys of the pianoforte. "I should return to Arthur," she said. "He does not fare well when distanced from me for a long time."

Henry watched her carefully. "Very well. It has been a busy day, and I—I ought to return to my study to work as well. Will I see you both at dinner at six o'clock?"

Eleanor noted his change of stance. She had never seen him appear less that perfectly confident, but he appeared somewhat defeated.

She simply nodded, not knowing what else to do. What was wrong with her? He was trying to be hospitable and she was making him uncomfortable.

Henry gave her a tight smile as he walked by, his boots

clicking on the floor. Every sound felt louder in this room, even the silence seemed to have its own sound—its own deafening sound. Why could she not behave normally around Henry? She did not mean to give the indication that she did not trust him, because she did. Didn't she? He had given her no reason not to. Bottled frustration collected in her chest, and she could hardly breathe. What a way to repay the man who had sacrificed so much for her.

She was not accustomed to people sacrificing things for her. She had sacrificed, and she had given, and all life had done to her was take. Life had taken her mother, her father, her peace, her innocence, and even parts of her personality. She did not know how to properly *receive*.

With a deep breath, she weaved her way past the various instruments and stepped into the hall. Henry was already gone.

When Eleanor returned to Arthur's room, he was still asleep. She sat on the edge of his bed, studying the light crease in his forehead. Such a young child should not have a crease like that, one she knew had been formed from constant worry and fear.

She hoped he could be happy with this new life fate had granted them.

She hoped she could too.

The hours passed slowly, and knots formed in Eleanor's stomach as she anticipated dinner with Henry. She was terrible at conversing—it had been too long since she had practiced. Even her first time speaking with him when he had saved their coach from the mud, she had behaved more normally than this. But that was before she fully noticed his blue eyes and golden hair and warm smile. Before he sacrificed much more than a meal and some spare change.

Arthur awoke with just enough time to change for dinner. Eleanor had very few gowns, but she wore one of the new ones, a pale blue, that she had found in town with Amelia in the week leading up to her wedding. She would have much to learn about running her own household, but for now, she simply walked down to the dining room, Arthur holding her hand. She was fortunate just to have remembered where the room was.

Henry stood when she entered, looking decidedly nervous. It did little to alleviate her own nervousness to see that he felt the same.

"Eleanor, Arthur, please sit down." Henry smiled, gesturing at two nearby chairs. "I trust you had an enjoyable afternoon?"

Eleanor nodded, sitting down at the table. "Yes. Arthur slept through most of it."

"Does he like the house?"

"He likes his bed at the very least."

Henry's lips quirked upward at the corners, his eyes flickering between Eleanor and Arthur. They settled on Arthur. "Do you like cake? I have asked the cook to bake one for dessert this evening to celebrate your first day at your new home."

Arthur blinked. "Cake?"

"We were not afforded such delicacies at our previous residence," Eleanor said. "Arthur has never tasted it."

Henry's expression bloomed with compassion. "You have never tasted cake?"

Arthur shook his head. "What does it taste wike?"

"Heaven on earth." Henry grinned, meeting Eleanor's eyes. "Would you agree?"

The last cake she had eaten would have had to have been the Brighton bakery's Shrewsbury cakes, her very favorite treat. Her mouth watered at the thought of the flaky, citrus infused cake. "Wholeheartedly," she said.

A gleam of excitement appeared in Arthur's eyes, and Henry winked at him. "I will make certain you receive a large slice of cake this evening."

Eleanor met his eyes with a grateful smile. Henry smiled back past the arms of the servants as they set the first course on the table.

"I hope to show you more of Worthing," he said. "It is a beautiful area, and I would even venture to say it rivals Brighton in beauty. The sea is nearby, the hills are greener, and our town shops are a bit quainter. You do enjoy shopping, don't you? I have not met a woman that abhors it."

Eleanor gave a soft smile. "Nor have I. I do enjoy it, very much."

"I hope to take you into town as soon as you wish to have new dresses made." Henry took a spoonful of his soup, and Eleanor took it as an opportunity to taste her own dish. The creamy soup burned on the way down. She swallowed hard, picking up her goblet to cool her throat.

"Is the soup too hot?" Henry asked, true concern in his voice.

"Not at all. I think it simply took me by surprise."

"I'd wager you have had a lot of surprise to deal with of late." Henry's eyes were gentle. "The soup is likely the least of your concern."

She had experienced more than her fair share. A scream cut through her mind, a flash of red, and a white sheet. She pushed the memory away, her stomach turning over and over. Her plate appeared suddenly unappetizing. She smiled, hoping Henry couldn't hear her heart pounding. Could she keep her secrets from him forever? She owed him the truth after all he had done for her, but she couldn't bring herself to tell anyone what had happened the day she left for Brighton. Fear mounted her spine, climbing up and up, wrapping around her like a snake.

All remnants of her smile had disappeared, and her stomach resisted every bite of soup. She did not feel inclined to speak, and after a few attempts at conversation, it seemed Henry felt the same. The rest of the meal was served in near silence, with a few remarks on the meal or the room offered on occasion. Arthur seemed to enjoy his cake, eating every last crumb, but Eleanor could hardly taste hers.

She took several moments to study Henry's face. Every feature was tight, uncomfortable, as he dragged his fork quietly over his plate. "Would you like to spend a few minutes in the drawing room?" he asked.

Eleanor nodded, relieved to have the silence broken and the meal over with. The sooner she could escape to her room, the better. In the dark days in the North, she had grown accustomed to being alone. She preferred being alone to sort through her emotions, her fears, and her troubled thoughts. Alone was where she found solutions, clarity, and strength. Arthur had often needed her, but she had not needed anyone.

She followed Henry through the shadowed hall, pulling Arthur along beside her. When Henry entered the drawing room, he turned around, his blue eyes flashing bright in the sudden light from the fireplace. "I thought Arthur might enjoy one of my favorite books." He walked to the coffee table, scooping up a thin volume.

He waited for Eleanor to sit before taking a seat on the settee to her right. He patted the cushion beside him, ushering Arthur forward. "I would like to read you a story," Henry said. "Come, sit."

Arthur glanced back at Eleanor as he walked tentatively forward. He sat down beside Henry, his feet dangling above the ground as he glanced at the cover of the book in Henry's hand.

"Mama tells me stories," Arthur said.

"Does she?" Henry's gaze lifted, and he raised his eyebrows at her. "Perhaps she will tell us one this evening."

Eleanor's stomach squeezed. "No, there will be no need for that."

"Please, Mama," Arthur said. His eyes, appearing every bit as large and blue as Henry's, stared at her mercilessly. "My favorite one."

She knew which one Arthur's favorite was. It was the story he asked for nearly every night. She had created the story to give herself hope when it had been the faintest. To recite the story for Henry would impose a level of vulnerability that terrified her. She clasped her hands tightly in her lap. "Perhaps another time."

Henry tipped his head to one side. "And deny me the opportunity to hear it?"

"Yes, that would be the point." She had meant it seriously, but the smile on Henry's face told her it had been interpreted otherwise.

His eyes flashed with amusement and he arched one eyebrow, watching her with his tell-tale curiosity. "What do you say, Arthur? Shall we ask her again once our book is finished? Do you think we shall change her mind?"

Arthur nodded, turning his attention back to the book in Henry's hand.

Eleanor grumbled inwardly. Her annoyance was quickly banished, however, when Henry began reading. His voice, deep and gentle, began relaying a story of three young lambs. The book was illustrated, but Arthur seemed uninterested in the pages. He was wholly captivated, as she was, by Henry. Arthur giggled at his expressions as he spoke for the characters, and she could see his little shoulders relaxing as the story went on. He even moved closer to Henry, unafraid to lean into his arm to obtain a closer look at the pictures.

Eleanor hardly heard the story. All she saw was the look of delight and peace on Arthur's face as Henry turned the last page, closing the book in his lap. Threads of warmth spread up her arms and through her heart as Henry smiled down at Arthur.

Her heart hammered and emotion gripped her throat. She tried her best to hide it. She was so moved by Arthur's expression that she needed something to hold onto. She clasped her hands so tightly together that her knuckles turned white. Henry turned his smile toward her, and the warmth in her chest caught fire.

"Mama's story now," Arthur said.

"What? No." Eleanor shook her head.

"Yes," Henry said. "Please."

Eleanor cursed the gentleness, the softness, the irresistibility of that *please*. She did not know how to refuse his simple request after all he had done for her. "Very well."

Henry sat back, crossing one leg over his knee, a pleased smile on his lips. Arthur mimicked his posture, glancing up at Henry to ensure he had done it right.

Another stab of emotion pricked at her throat. She had hoped and prayed that Arthur would not become like his father, but here was a man that she would be quite pleased for him to grow up to be like. Her heart skipped with admiration for Henry, despite her every intention not to feel it. She was seconds away from becoming a watering pot, she was certain of it. Her tears seemed to balance on her lower eyelids.

Somehow, she managed to keep her emotions in their proper place, but only just. She tried to keep her voice steady as she began her story.

Arthur listened intently, and so did Henry.

"Deep within the trees, where the leaves grew dark and the sun never shined, lived a young boy," she began. "He had lived his entire life there, in the cold and in the dark, but a doe of the forest told him tales of a world beyond his own, a world with light and warmth. At first, the boy did not believe her. *How could there be such a thing as light?* he asked. *Light is there*, the deer said. *One day it will find you.*"

Henry watched her, the intensity of his gaze sending her voice out of rhythm.

She swallowed her anxiety. She looked at Arthur as she spoke, pretending Henry was not there at all. "The boy waited, watching for signs of the light. He had never seen it, so he did not know what to watch for. In the days he waited, the boy proved his strength, fighting the monsters that passed through his land, waiting at the edge of the stream for the day the light would find them. He knew it would come one day, but he did not know when."

"Can I say the next part?" Arthur asked.

Eleanor nodded.

"*When will the light come?*" Arthur recited, speaking for the boy of the story.

She smiled softly, speaking for the doe. "*It does not matter when it comes, but it matters that it will come. We must prepare to receive it.* In search of the light, the boy and the deer cut down the trees surrounding their stream, revealing the moon in the sky. *It is just night that causes this darkness*, the deer said. *Day always follows night*. When the last of the trees were cleared, tiny flecks appeared beside the moon. *Those are the stars*, the deer said. *They are the footprints of light. We must follow them*. The deer and the boy crossed the stream, walked through the woods, climbed the mountains, and came to a meadow filled with beautiful dark flowers. Exhausted from their journey, the boy and the deer lay down among the flowers.

"*Is this where the light lives?*" Arthur said, his voice quick, continuing the story.

"The deer had begun to wonder, like the boy, whether light was real. *If light lives in you, and it lives in me, no matter where we go or what we face, we shall always have light*, the deer said. As the words were spoken, the sky turned pink, then peach, then yellow. The sun rose above the mountains, spilling warmth onto the flowers and the boy and the deer. Colors grew vibrant, and a path appeared before them. *The light has given us a path*, the deer said.

Eleanor paused so Arthur could speak his part. "*Where does the path lead?*" Arthur said, his voice filled with excitement.

Eleanor took a deep breath, one meant to fortify her. "It will lead us home."

The room settled in silence, and she dared a glance at Henry's face. She was so surprised by the warmth and emotion she saw, that she had to look away. All she knew were her father's ever-collected expressions, Adam's that were the same, and her late husband's cold stares. At that moment, she realized something she hadn't fully realized since meeting Henry. He had a soft heart. Is that what had compelled him to save her and Arthur? To marry her that day? Was it truly as simple as that?

She fought her own emotions with a firm grip, keeping

them tucked away. She looked down, hoping to lighten the heaviness of the room. "It is a strange story."

"No," Henry's voice was quiet. "It is a beautiful story."

Her gaze hovered over his for several seconds. "Thank you." She could not gather the strength to look away. She wanted to believe that he was the source of light that had saved her and Arthur, that would keep them safe forever. He was her husband. Wasn't that what a husband was supposed to do? She had learned the opposite to be true with Mr. Quinton, but there was a stark difference between darkness and light. For the first time in years, she felt as if she were finally surrounded by light once again. Even if it wasn't what she had planned for herself, it seemed fate had granted her a different plan. Henry.

Her legs shook as she stood. She needed to be alone to sort through her emotions. She walked to the settee and took Arthur's hand. "It is time we retired for the evening. Thank you for the meal and for—for everything."

Henry smiled up at her, and the wick in her chest caught fire once again. How could he affect her so much with a simple smile? She felt she hardly knew the man. She cursed her pounding heart, attempting to appear unaffected.

"Please, do not thank me," he said. "All that is mine is all yours. Never hesitate to ask for anything."

"Thank you."

He glanced up, a teasing glint in his eye. "I said you need not thank me."

Eleanor smiled. "Right. I am sorry."

"You need not apologize for thanking me either."

She bit her lip. "Good heavens, I have a lot to learn, don't I?"

He chuckled, a deep, musical sound. She wished it

would never stop. She loved to laugh but had not found a reason to laugh in a long while.

Henry patted Arthur's back as he stood, standing up beside him. Eleanor was reminded yet again of how very tall Henry was, how broad his chest and shoulders were, and the faint smell of soap and fresh linen on his clothes. "I will walk you both to your rooms."

Henry picked up the nearby candlestick and led the way. Eleanor followed Henry down the hall and up the stairs. The house, in all its vast hallways, had an eerie feeling at night. She had never spent a night in such a large house. And this house was hers. It would take a long time for that thought to fully sink in, as well as the thought that *Henry* was hers.

They entered Arthur's room, where the bed had been remade. Henry's candle provided just enough light to see a faint outline of the rocking horse by the far window.

Eleanor turned to Henry. "He needs me here when he falls asleep. He gets quite frightened, and I do not know how he will be in a new house."

Henry nodded. "Your room is just across the hall, as you already know." He gave a small smile. "Do not hesitate to call Mary with any assistance you may need. She has unpacked your things and arranged them in your room. I hope it all is to your liking."

"I am sure it will be." She refrained from thanking him, knowing it would bring about another round of teasing.

Henry turned to Arthur, bending down to put his hand on his shoulder. "Goodnight."

Arthur smiled, just a shy lift of his lips. "Goodnight."

Henry straightened, his gaze meeting Eleanor's. "Goodnight."

Her voice sounded so weak and soft next to Henry's

strong one when she said goodnight back.

Henry set the candle on the table beside Arthur's bed, leaving them with one last smile as he closed the door behind him. Eleanor stared at the closed door for several seconds before beginning her search for Arthur's night clothes among his unpacked trunk. After helping him get ready for bed, she tucked him beneath his blankets.

"What do you think of your new home?" Eleanor asked, folding the blanket beneath his chin. He pressed his chin down, keeping his neck away from her fingers. He had always been a ticklish one.

"I wike it," he whispered.

"Do you like Mr. Beaumont?" Eleanor asked. She held her breath.

A small smile spread onto Arthur's cheeks. "Yes." He rolled onto his side, nestling into his pillow. He yawned. "Will you sing me a song?" His request had come often, but for the first time, it had not come with any indication of fear, of a need to be comforted.

She smoothed back his dark hair, running her fingertips over his closed eyelids as she sang.

Hush, rest your head
The rain will end
The cracks will mend
The clouds will part
Rest aching hearts.

Hush, close your eyes
The sun will rise
The robin sings
Of happy things
Of days ahead.

AN UNEXPECTED BRIDE

Hush, fall asleep
The past we'll keep
Let future reap
A spring to hold
A joy like gold

Chapter 9

Henry heard Eleanor singing almost every night, a tune he had never heard before. He had never been one for eavesdropping, but he had listened to every word. Among Eleanor's growing list of fine attributes, Henry could now add singing.

A week had passed since their wedding, and he felt he was finally coming to know her a little better. Their conversations mostly consisted of matters of business as he taught her about the estate and the income it brought in, and the responsibilities she would have as hostess. They planned to invite her family to come for dinner often, and he hoped to introduce her to the neighbors as soon as she was comfortable.

He rarely saw Eleanor outside of meal times, for she and Arthur often explored the grounds and house without him. He did not need an invitation, but he would have liked one. He felt bothersome to request to join them. They were adjusting to their new home, and he needed to stay out of it. He simply wished Eleanor would *care* to see him. He had not realized his frustrations on the matter until he had come to his fencing room that morning.

He raised his epee and advanced on his opponent, Silas, his valet.

This fencing match took even less time than usual, considering Henry always fought harder when there was a great deal on his mind. He disarmed Silas within two minutes, driving him against the wall and pressing the tip of his epee against his chest. Silas lifted his mask, a broad grin on his face.

"You've gotten better, sir. I wish I could give ye more of a fight." He wiped a bead of perspiration from his forehead. "Yer brother's the only one I've seen give ye a challenge."

Henry smiled, lifting his own mask. Even so, Henry could count less than five times that Edward had bested him. Fencing had always been Henry's talent.

Here at his estate in Worthing, Silas had proved the best competitor of all Henry's servants, and an even better friend and confidant. Henry had known Silas growing up in Brighton. Born to a lower-class family, Silas had been in search of work. When Henry inherited the estate, he had offered Silas a position as valet.

"How does yer wife like the house?" Silas asked.

Henry rubbed one side of his face. "I—I believe she likes it. In truth, I cannot entirely decipher her opinions. She rarely speaks them. She is a very difficult woman to understand." Henry could not put it any other way. Eleanor *was* difficult to understand, and so was the draw he felt to her. At one moment she was detached and distant, and at another, she smiled and appeared comfortable. He wanted her to always feel the latter, but he did not know how to put her at ease. Surely so much change was difficult for her to bear. It was difficult for him. He wanted Arthur to feel comfortable with him too, and it seemed he was already making progress on that matter.

"Does yer wife like *you*?" Silas asked. His freckles seemed to move when he smiled, dancing along with the teasing glint in his eyes.

"What is not to like?" Henry smiled, stretching his neck and setting down his epee. He took a drink of water from his cup as Silas chuckled.

Henry sighed. "In truth, I do not know. I cannot read her opinions if she will not state them aloud. Her face is of a most…stoic sort." Stoic, but still lovely. The few glimpses he had seen of her smile had left him rather battered. He wondered how she would appear with a full smile, not just a whisper of one. He could not blame her for being stoic. She had endured so much. She had every right to be afraid and to be cautious. All he could do was be patient and try his hardest to earn her trust.

"Yer a saint fer taking them in," Silas said.

"I married her," Henry said. "I did not just take them in. She and her son are now my family."

"Right. That makes ye even more of a saint, I'd say."

Henry was tired of being called a saint, for being praised for what he did. It was what any man with a conscience might have done, and he answered to nothing if not his conscience. He was a slave to it. He was fairly certain he could not do something wicked if it would save his life. He would wallow in guilt for the remainder of his days. To marry Eleanor had not been a difficult choice. It had been his only choice. To love her… he did not know how to choose that. Grace had made it sound so easy. How could he love her if she did not love him in return? Was it even worth trying?

"I want to make them feel at home here," Henry said, reminding himself of his most important goal. "I gather that they have had a very difficult life. I wish for them to leave it all behind. I wish for them to be as happy as they deserve to be. But the problem of the matter is… I haven't the slightest idea of what makes a woman happy." Henry paced the room with his cup, thinking.

Silas shrugged. "I'd wager she needs female companionship. My sisters were always happiest with a group of ladies in the sitting room and a tray of tea in front of them. Content as a cat with a bird between its paws, they were." Silas nodded to emphasize his words.

Henry considered the idea. "Yes. I think you may be right."

"Am I ever wrong?"

"Yes, more often than not." Henry tossed him a smile. "But—I believe that idea holds merit."

Silas chuckled.

Henry knew his neighbors just a half-mile south to be a household of ladies. He would invite the mother and her two daughters to tea the next day if Eleanor liked the idea. He would speak with her on the matter as soon as possible.

"I suspect she would also enjoy a bit of frivolity," Silas added. "You might host a party or secure an invitation to one."

Henry did not know how much Eleanor would enjoy *frivolity*, but he took note of the idea as he left the room.

Once he was washed and changed, he crossed the hall to the breakfast room, finding it empty. As he passed the back door, he glanced out the window. Eleanor and Arthur were in the gardens, examining a rose bush. He walked out to join them, weaving through the shrubs and trees to where he knew the yellow rose bush to be located. They had not seen him yet, and he paused to observe them before making himself known.

"These are wike the flowers in your story, Mama." Arthur's little voice was much louder and more confident than Henry had ever heard it.

"Yes, they are." He could hear the smile in Eleanor's voice. Why didn't she smile around him? "Is yellow your favorite color?"

Arthur nodded, giggling. "How did you know, Mama?"

She laughed.

Laughed. Henry had not known she was capable of it.

Devil take it. He would earn a laugh from her eventually if it was the last thing he did. He stopped a few feet behind them. "Would you like a rose?"

Both Eleanor and her son jumped, whirling to face him.

He held up his hands. "It is only me, not to worry." He smiled, hoping to erase the surprise and fear on their faces. Good heavens, they were a jumpy pair. He took in Eleanor's appearance—her black hair piled atop her head, with few curls left unpinned, and she wore no bonnet. He liked the style, for it gave him a clearer view of her entire face. She wore a pale pink morning dress, the sleeves reaching to her elbows, the bodice trimmed with white. Her pale skin provided a stark contrast to her hair and lips, and her blue eyes were striking.

She shifted, her cheeks growing slightly pink at the centers to match her dress.

He tore his gaze away, cursing himself for making her

even more uncomfortable by staring so unabashedly at her. How had he not noticed her beauty before?

"I am sorry to have startled you." He smiled, turning his gaze to Arthur. "Would you like a flower?"

"No. But Mama wants one."

Eleanor shook her head, half her mouth lifting upward. "No, I would not have such a lovely thing plucked away from all its friends. Look, it is so happy." She pointed at the nearest rose, nestled among the leaves with all the others. Henry observed the whimsical expression on Eleanor's face, wondering how often it came, or how long it would last. He was beginning to learn that Eleanor liked symbolism. The story she had told the week before had taught him as much.

He tried to decipher all he could from her words. *Plucked away from all its friends.* Was she feeling much like a rose, plucked from a bush it called home? By marrying her he had taken her from Brighton, the home she had been longing for for so many years. Perhaps it wasn't just new female companions and friends that would make her happy, but her old ones as well. He would invite her family to dinner soon or take her to visit them.

Henry stepped closer, joining Eleanor and Arthur in their study of the flowers. "You are right. We shall not pluck any roses. I see the wisdom in leaving them here. Why take just one rose away to your room to admire it there, when you could come visit this bush each day, and see dozens of them?"

Eleanor touched one of the petals, staring lovingly at it. "I did not have flowers like this in the North. There was little to admire besides prickly moors."

He studied her profile. "I will have even more planted if you wish."

"I am quite happy with just these flowers." She glanced up at him briefly before returning her gaze to the rose. She lowered her nose to the bud, inhaling deeply.

Henry turned to Arthur, bending down slightly to be closer to his height. His black hair fell over his ears and forehead, nearly covering his eyes. He would need to arrange a haircut for the boy. "Your mother has her roses. What is it *you* would like today, Arthur?"

Arthur shrugged, his large blue eyes squinting against the sun.

An idea struck Henry. "I told you I had tigers, did I not?"

Arthur's eyes flashed with misgiving. "I don't want one."

"I thought so. Would you prefer kittens?"

Arthur nodded fast. "I wike kittens."

Henry's neighbors had a cat that had just delivered a new litter of kittens the month before, and he knew that at least three kittens remained in need of a home. He had not interacted too closely with Mrs. Morton and her daughters, but he thought they could possibly provide Eleanor with the female companionship Silas had suggested she needed. Mr. Morton was agreeable, so the women of his family were likely agreeable too.

"I happen to know three kittens in need of a new friend. Would you like to see them today?" Henry asked Arthur.

He glanced at Eleanor to ensure she agreed to the plan. There was nothing in her face that showed protest, so he took it as encouragement. "It isn't far. Would you be opposed to walking?"

Eleanor shook her head. "I love to walk."

"Perfect." Henry smiled, and Eleanor took his outstretched arm. The Morton's residence took only ten minutes to reach. The housekeeper informed them that Mrs. Morton and her daughters had taken a trip into town and would return shortly, but she gladly led them to the place where the kittens were kept under the shade of a bush in the gardens.

"You ought to take one of them home," the housekeeper said. "The master doesn't know what to do with them. He can't keep 'em all."

Henry watched with amusement as Arthur took tentative steps toward the kittens. Two of the kittens were black, and one was black with white paws. Arthur sat down on the grass, reaching out to touch the velvet ears of the nearest kitten. The housekeeper knelt on the grass near him, introducing him to each cat and helping him hold one in his lap.

"Arthur loves cats," Eleanor said, her abrupt words catching Henry by surprise. He glanced down at her. Though her voice was soft, it was sharp and clear. He never mistook her words. Her voice was slightly deeper than the average woman, but still feminine. He liked the sound of it. He had grown tired of shrill laughter and conversations with women that enjoyed being heard above their companions.

Eleanor looked as if she were about to say more, so Henry simply nodded, listening.

"We had a cat once," she continued. "Mr. Quinton brought her home shortly after Arthur learned to walk, hoping the cat would keep Arthur preoccupied in his room for more of the day. I named her Petal." She smiled lightly. "She brought a great deal of joy to our lives."

Henry watched her expression fade to a fearful one, the spark of joy at the memory diminishing in her eyes.

"What happened to her?" Henry asked, keeping his voice gentle.

Eleanor took an audible breath, rubbing her palms

over her skirts. "Mr. Quinton decided…he would rather have a dog. I never discovered what he did to Petal, and I do not like to dwell on it. But one day Petal was simply gone." Eleanor's eyes flickered up to his. "Arthur was heartbroken. The dog was large and not well-trained, and Arthur was afraid of him."

Henry moved his gaze to Arthur, where he sat in the grass, rubbing the black and white kitten's tail between two fingers, giggling.

Taking their cat was just the beginning of the harm Mr. Quinton had done before his death. It was likely only a small part of the things he had taken from them. Henry felt his jaw clenching. Anger roiled inside him, burning hot. "I wish I could have been there to protect you from him."

Eleanor's brow furrowed. "From the dog?"

"No. From your late husband." Henry met her eyes.

She looked down at the ground. "I wish it too. But you have offered us a way to escape, and that is more than I can ever thank you for."

Henry had given a lot of thought to the day he saw Eleanor on her journey back to Brighton. Why had she lied to him about her husband's death? He sensed that she was still hiding something. What other reason could she have had to lie to him? His curiosity burned with questions regarding her husband's death and the elder Mr. Quinton's threats and accusations, but he couldn't bring himself to ask for answers. At least not yet. He did not wish to scare Eleanor away when she was finally speaking to him.

"Remember," he said, offering a teasing smile, "you do not need to thank me for anything."

She smiled at the ground, and he wished she would look up at him. "Am I truly not allowed to utter those words?"

He shook his head before realizing she couldn't see it. "You are allowed to do anything you wish—you do not need my permission."

"You deserve gratitude. I have to give it somehow."

Henry rubbed his chin. "You may show your gratitude by joining me for a ride tomorrow morning? My morning rides are rather lonely at present, and I want to take every opportunity to come to know you better."

Eleanor met his eyes, a spark of hope entering them. "It has been far too long since I have ridden. I enjoy being around the animals."

"Are you saying yes?"

Another half-smile lifted her lips, and Henry found himself enchanted by it. "Yes."

He held her gaze for a long moment, his own smile growing. He had never seen Eleanor this comfortable beside him. It was progress, to be sure.

"Mr. Beaumont, how do you do?" A woman's voice met his ears from across the lawn. Strolling along the garden path with her two daughters, was Mrs. Morton. She was a woman of very particular fashion, always wearing the most recent trend and instructing her daughters to do the same. Their gowns appeared to coordinate in color, with each woman donning a peach accessory. Mrs. Morton wore a peach gown, Miss Morton a peach trimmed bonnet, and Miss Beatrice a peach shawl. Mrs. Morton's smile appeared much less jovial than usual, her greeting less enthusiastic.

"Good morning, Mrs. Morton." Henry said.

She came to a stop in front of them, her eyes lingering on Eleanor before returning to Henry.

He felt he should provide an explanation as to why they were on her property without invitation. "Your housekeeper said you would not be home. I hope we are not imposing. I wished to introduce my stepson to the kittens."

Mrs. Morton exchanged a glance with her nearest daughter. "Your stepson?" Her eyebrows flew upwards, her green eyes flashing with surprise. "I had heard of your recent marriage, of course, for the whole town has been speaking of it, but I did not realize it came with a child." Her eyes flicked to Arthur, where he sat with the kittens.

Henry sensed Eleanor grow tense beside him.

"Yes. He is a very well-behaved, kind boy. I am honored to have him, as well as my new wife." He smiled, fully noticing the disdain that dripped from Mrs. Morton's expressions. He slid his arm around Eleanor's elbow. She stepped forward, her smile shaky as she greeted Mrs. Morton with a nod.

"Mrs. Beaumont," Mrs. Morton returned the nod, but with less depth, "I have heard so very much about you."

Henry's chest tightened. Whatever Mrs. Morton had heard could not have been complimentary. The news of the missing Claridge girl had once been a very exciting topic of gossip, and even more so when the public heard of the scandalous elopement connected to it. Henry had known upon marrying Eleanor that his own reputation would suffer, and quite frankly, he did not care what Mrs. Morton and her small circles of friends thought of him or Eleanor.

Eleanor surprised him by speaking. "What have you heard concerning me?"

Mrs. Morton's eyes widened in surprise. "Well, I—" she fluttered her hands. "Much. I have heard much."

"I am curious as to what that means." Eleanor tipped her head to one side. She appeared genuinely curious, but Henry sensed a challenge in her eyes.

Mrs. Morton's pride bristled, visible in the straightening of her shoulders and the huffed breath she let loose. "Very well. I have heard that you entered into a scandalous elopement with a poor soldier, leaving behind your family, and leaving them to wonder over your whereabouts. Your husband must have died, it seems, for you to have married Mr. Beaumont. I am shocked to see that you have married again so quickly and are already out of mourning. As I said, I have heard much."

Henry's anger mounted again. "I'm afraid you are wrong, Mrs. Morton," he said. "There is much that you do not know concerning my new family."

Her eyes flashed. "Oh, I do not blame you for attempting to subdue the rumors surrounding your wife, Mr. Beaumont. Your own reputation is suffering as a result of hers."

His jaw tightened. "The rumors you have heard are false."

Mrs. Morton raised her chin. "I must rely on what I have heard to formulate my opinions of my new neighbors."

Eleanor's voice came again, strong and inarguable. "To rely on gossip is to rely on uncertainty. The one who relies on truth will be both wiser and provide more pleasant company."

Mrs. Morton scoffed. "There is nothing uncertain about your reputation, my dear. Nothing can mend it. You will take Mr. Beaumont with you as you continue to fall in society. I was sorely disappointed to hear of his marriage to you."

"Have you no interest in learning the truth?" Henry wished he could throw the woman off the property, but the property belonged, in fact, to Mrs. Morton. He had never known the woman to be so condescending and rude.

"The truth? The truth is that you will never be the esteemed son of an earl that you were born to be. You have been ruined by your association with this woman."

Eleanor flinched, her posture slackening. Henry's gaze hardened. He needed to get away from Mrs. Morton now, before he did something that would ensure Silas and Edward never called him a 'saint' again. He took Eleanor's hand, his heart sinking when he felt it trembling.

"Arthur," Henry said, exhausting all his effort to keep his voice calm. "It is time to leave."

The boy seemed to sense the tension around him, standing up quickly and taking hold of his mother's other arm. He stared back at the kittens as they walked away.

Henry held his composure, but only just. How dare Mrs. Morton say those things? He had never met a person with such disregard for the feelings of others. Eleanor, who just moments ago had been smiling, now appeared far from it.

The walk back to the house passed in silence. Henry needed to give his anger a chance to subside before he spoke. By the time the house appeared in the distance, he trusted himself to speak.

"I am sorry, Eleanor. I did not know Mrs. Morton to be so dreadful."

"She is dreadful, isn't she?" Eleanor avoided his eyes again, as if she were afraid to be near him again. She held tightly to Arthur's hand.

Blast Mrs. Morton.

"Please do not believe a word that she said."

Something like exhaustion appeared on Eleanor's face, clouding her features. "She spoke some truth. I have ruined you. Society will not know you as the respectable son of an earl. They will know you as the husband to the scandalous Claridge girl." Her voice cracked. "I am the one that should be sorry."

"Do not apologize. You have done nothing wrong."

Her eyes glinted. "Yes." Her voice softened, shaking, as if she were making a confession. "I have."

They had reached the back door, and she took Arthur by the hand. "I do not feel well."

With that, she opened the door, walking swiftly past it and out of sight.

Henry watched the door close behind her, wondering yet again what it was that she was hiding from him.

Chapter 10

Eleanor rushed up the stairs, her breath hitching and catching just like her skirts under her boots. She picked up Arthur, who remained silent, lines of worry creasing his forehead. She tried to keep her expression even, but Arthur always knew when something was wrong. And something was very wrong, indeed.

As luck would have it, Mary was in Arthur's room, making his bed. "May I leave Arthur to play with you for a few minutes?" Eleanor asked.

She nodded, apparently sensing Eleanor's distress. Eleanor set Arthur down to his feet, gently prodding him toward Mary, who took his hand.

She did not wish for him to see her in such an uncollected state. She bit back her tears just until she crossed the threshold of her own room, closing the door firmly behind her. It would be just a moment. It would take just a moment for her to recollect herself. It always took *just a moment.*

Eleanor breathed deeply, Mrs. Morton's words echoing through her skull over and over. Had Eleanor known what the consequences would be to Henry, she never would have let him marry her. He would grow to resent her for what she did to him. And if it was ever discovered what she did to her late husband…then Henry would be ruined for certain. She had almost told him, but then she had been too afraid. She did not want to put him in even more danger by giving him her secrets to protect.

She sat down on the edge of her bed, trying to calm her breathing. A knock sounded at the door, and she froze. She had come to recognize Mary's knock, and this one was not the same.

"Eleanor?"

Henry's voice. Her heart leapt.

"Yes?"

"May I come in?"

She crossed the room to the door, pulling it open. The sorrow and regret in Henry's eyes was unmistakable. Was he already regretting his decision to marry her? She would not blame him for it. She hid her emotions, crossing her arms as he walked slowly into the room.

"Are you still unwell?" he asked, his voice so soft and gentle she felt a strange urge to run to him, to bury her face in his chest and cry like she hadn't in years. She shook the feeling away.

"Yes, I am much better. I am just—not accustomed to the heat of summer."

Henry threw her a skeptical look but did not press her for an honest explanation. She liked that about him.

"There is something that I wish to say." Henry's voice

was slow, as if to ensure she would not possibly miss a word. "I must clarify at once that you have not ruined me. Not in the slightest." He stared into her eyes, his own gaze firm and resolute. "You have saved me. You and Arthur have both saved me from a life of loneliness and monotony, and for that I must express my gratitude to you."

She didn't know how to respond. The threads of warmth that had grown all too familiar spread up her limbs and into her chest.

He walked closer, and her heart picked up speed. His closeness always had an effect on her, whether it was a sense of security or belonging, or the strange feelings he had begun to stir up in her heart. She scolded her heart for caring about his words, for believing them. Hadn't she learned not to trust flattering words?

No. Words could not be trusted. Only actions could. Henry's actions had shown that he was noble in every way, yet she still hesitated to tell him everything. She was still afraid to let him close to her, to believe that he would not abandon her and Arthur when they needed him most. She squeezed her eyes shut against the memories that tore at her composure.

Without warning, Henry's fingers touched her cheek. Her eyes flew open and she flinched, pulling away and stumbling back a step.

Henry's hand fell, his eyes flashing with hurt. He appeared embarrassed, and Eleanor's stomach twisted with guilt. She hadn't meant to act so afraid of him, but the instinct had come naturally.

"I will leave you," Henry said, his voice quiet. "I hope you feel well again soon."

Before she could try to explain, he turned around, exiting her room without another word.

She pressed her palm to her forehead, fighting tears all over again. Henry did all he could to leave a wake of kindness and compassion behind him, in every word and deed. It seemed all she was capable of was leaving a wake of destruction in her path.

***

A candidate for Arthur's nursemaid arrived a week later for an interview. Her name was Adeline, and she was quite young. If Eleanor would have guessed the girl's age, she would have thought her to be sixteen, with her youthful eyes and small frame. Even so, she seemed quite capable of performing the needed duties, and with her quiet, calm disposition, Eleanor thought Arthur would be quite comfortable around her.

With Arthur now in Adeline's care in the early mornings, Eleanor had taken to spending her mornings in the gardens. She was not used to having time to herself out of doors, but she found she quite enjoyed it. She loved listening to the birds and inhaling the fragrant scents of the nearby rose bushes. She felt at peace there in the gardens. Her stone bench surrounded by trees and bushes had become something of a sanctuary.

While outside one morning, Eleanor was presented with a letter. Her heart skittered with fear before she saw who it had come from.

Adam.

She tore open the seal, eager to hear from him. She was disappointed to see that it was quite short.

Dear Eleanor,

I hope you are happy in Worthing and that Mr. Beaumont is treating you and Arthur well. My wife and I have received an invitation to a dinner party on the tenth at the residence of the Marquess of Seaford. Do you remember my old friend Philip Honeyfield? He is now a marquess and has a grand estate, which is likely the very last thing I would have imagined for his life to turn into. He has invited many of our friends from Brighton and he was more than happy to extend his invitation to include you and Mr. Beaumont. I need to see you again, Eleanor, to ensure you are happy and safe. I hope you will come. I believe Mr. Beaumont will know where to find Philip's estate, Pengrave, in Seaford.

*With love,
Adam*

Eleanor held the letter to her chest. Could she ask Henry to take her to the party? He had told her never to hesitate to ask for anything. Part of her was still afraid to venture outside of Worthing. What if the elder Mr. Quinton found her? She reminded herself that the dinner party was being held in Seaford, so there would be no risk of being discovered by Mr. Quinton there. Had he already been searching for her? The thoughts sent prickles of dread over her spine.

"Good morning."

She jumped at the sound of Henry's voice.

He was walking down the path toward her bench, each step tentative and cautious. "It seems I have made a habit of startling you." He chuckled, but the sound was half-hearted. She and Henry had hardly spoken since the week before, when he had touched her face and she had pulled away as if it had disgusted her. She hadn't meant to offend or hurt him, and the persistent guilt that had followed her all week was enough to drive her mad. She needed to show him that she did not fear him.

"It is not you that is startling me," she said, turning her face up to look at him. Sunlight fell softly through the trees, illuminating the golden tones in Henry's hair and the streaks of pale blue in his eyes. "It is Mr. Quinton. My memories of him. My fear of his father." She shook her head. "It is not you."

Henry sat down beside her. She looked down at her hands, afraid she would cry if she looked at his face, at the gentle kindness in his eyes. She still felt that she needed to explain her reaction to his touch, why it had been so startling.

"Mr. Quinton hurt me on more than one occasion." She took a deep breath. "He never touched my face… unless to strike my cheek. He never touched me unless it was for his own purposes, his own desires, to hurt, to take, to control. And the only words he spoke to me were threats, followed by flattery that was meant to appease me."

She dared to look up at Henry's face. His jaw was tight with anger, his eyes heavy with sorrow. She clung to the expression, knowing that it meant he cared. She had never confided in anyone about the things she had felt and endured over those years. The daily battle with fear and deciding whether to fight or submit to her husband's demands.

How different Henry was from Mr. Quinton. She could not think of one similarity between them in either appearance or character, except, perhaps, the color of their eyes. Both men had blue eyes, but the color was where the similarity ended. Mr. Quinton's eyes had bled with darkness, and Henry's emitted light. Her heart pounded at the realization. She clung to Henry's light, to his nearness, to the feeling of trust that had begun growing in her heart. Even if he regretted marrying her, of taking her reputation upon him, at least she knew he cared about her.

He slipped his hand around hers, and she didn't flinch, didn't pull away. Her eyes fluttered closed as a tear escaped, spilling down her cheek. She took a shuddering breath.

"Eleanor," Henry's voice, soft, hoarse met her ears. She didn't dare open her eyes. She couldn't. His hand, warm and strong, enveloped hers tighter. "You must know that I will never, *never*, hurt you or Arthur."

Her closed eyelids were not enough to contain her tears. They slipped out the corners of her eyes and down her cheeks. Peace like she had not known in years enveloped her, born from Henry's words and voice and gentle touch. "I know."

She opened her eyes, Henry's face blurred behind the moisture in her vision, and she blinked to see him more clearly. His other hand lifted, slowly, carefully, until his fingers barely touched her cheek. She froze.

He shifted, his gaze concentrating on each of her features as he traced his thumb over her tears, soaking them up and stealing them away. "Do not cry," he whispered.

Her face burned under his touch, a barren flame flickering in her chest as she studied his face. The dark sweep of lashes, the faint stubble on his cheeks, the creases near his eyes from years of smiling, the golden curls that fell softly on his forehead. She tried to memorize it all, because a small part of her still feared she would lose him.

She had been schooled to believe that that which can be taken, will be taken, it is only a matter of time. Love, she had learned, was a weakness. And Henry was difficult not to love.

His eyes settled on hers, and a small smile curved his lips. Her heart fluttered at the sight of it. She would have been quite content to stay on that bench forever, surrounded by warm sunlight beside Henry.

"I came to see if you would still like to take the ride we planned last week," he said.

She had forgotten all about the ride. "I would." She smiled, the action much easier now. "Also," she turned to where she had placed the letter beside her, sniffing away the last of her tears, "I received an invitation from Adam to dine at Pengrave with the Marquess of Seaford in a fortnight. Would you like to go?"

Henry smiled. "Yes, of course. But only if you will sing."

"Sing?" Eleanor's eyes flew open.

"I hear you each night with Arthur as you help him to fall asleep. I would venture to say your singing is the loveliest sound I have ever heard."

"It cannot possibly be."

He glanced upward, as if reconsidering it. "Very well. It is second only to the sound of Mr. Fifett's compliments of my food and the huffed sound Mrs. Morton makes when she is offended."

A laugh bubbled out of Eleanor's chest. Just days ago, the topic of Mrs. Morton had not been even remotely humorous. She put a hand against her stomach, surprised by the uncontrollable laughter that struck her.

"Now I must amend my statement." Henry's smile grew wider. "Your singing is my favorite sound, second only to the sound of your laughter."

Eleanor's cheeks ached as she pressed her smile down to a reasonable size. "I'm sorry. I do not know what came over me."

"You must never apologize for laughing and smiling." He crossed one leg over his knee. "The world needs more of that. It already has plenty of scowls and frowns." He cast her a sideways smile of his own, setting her heart kicking and pounding all over again.

"Sometimes there are many reasons to scowl and frown," Eleanor said.

Henry studied her, sadness flashing over his face for a moment before a smile overtook it again. "When you have a reason to smile, take advantage of it. I have every reason to smile when I look at you."

Eleanor felt her cheeks grow warm, and she looked down.

"First, you make me smile when you do that." Henry chuckled.

"Do what?"

"Look down at your hands as if they are the most interesting object in the universe." She had known him to be observant, but not so observant as this. "Or when you lift your chin with inquisition, as if you are offering an unspoken challenge." He had leaned closer to her.

Eleanor glanced up at him from under her lashes. "I am quite observant too, you know."

"Are you?"

"Yes. You have the most curious stare I have ever seen."

"A curious stare?" He raised one eyebrow.

"Yes, just like that. You are curious as to what the 'curious stare' is, yet you are effecting it right now."

Henry laughed, resting his back against the bench. "Well, I *am* curious."

"Always. But you do not always ask questions. It is as if you enjoy the process of wondering." Eleanor turned to face him more fully. "I suspect you ponder over many things in your mind but hesitate to ask questions because you are afraid of causing offense."

"There are enough people in the world willing and ready to cause offense. I do not wish to take part in it. I'm certain I have caused offense to more than one person in my life, but never intentionally, and I believe that makes all the difference."

"Surely Mrs. Morton was offended by our words last week," Eleanor said. She threw a guilty glance at Henry, and he laughed.

"I will cause offense to anyone if it is done to defend your honor. That is the exception."

She still could not fully comprehend why he showed such kindness to her and Arthur from the very first moment he met them. She stared at him, trying to decipher the answer in his eyes.

"Is that the curious stare you accused me of?" He asked, eyeing her with suspicion.

She looked down, taking no effort to hide her smile. "I was just thinking about what could have made you so kind. You are the most selfless person I have ever met."

It was his turn to look down at his hands. Eleanor's heart skipped with admiration at the humility on his face, as if he were embarrassed by her praise. "My mother taught me from a young age that the best thing you can do to find your own happiness is to help others find theirs. The best way you can succeed is if you first help others succeed. The best way you can shine in society is if you give others the chance to shine first." He stared at the tree ahead, as if lost in his memories. "My older brother and I have always been very different. My father never paid heed to either of us. Edward did all he could to get his attention, and when he failed, he sought attention elsewhere. My father was not pleased. I took my mother's advice and spoke to my father often about Edward's strengths of character, hoping it would endear my father to Edward. I did all I could to help Edward succeed, yet I found no success of my own. Our father did not care for either of us as a father should."

He turned his gaze to her. "Though I began to doubt my mother's words, I have never stopped trying to live them. And I have finally seen the truth behind them with you and Arthur. It is my dearest wish for you both to be happy here. Since you have come, *I* have never been happier."

It eased a burden inside of her to hear those words. Henry was happy. He did not care about the disdain of society that she had brought him.

Deep inside her mind, fear still lay in wait, prepared to strike at any moment. She pushed it away. What would Henry think when he discovered the lie she had been telling? How could he be happy then?

"I am happy here," she said, ignoring the gnawing fear in her stomach. "Arthur is happy here too."

"I am glad to hear it. I hope I do not still frighten him."

"Not at all. I believe you have endeared yourself to him quite well. His trust is not easily won."

Henry smiled. "I hope to be a good father to him."

Eleanor had no doubt that Henry would be. The hope of her future made her heart soar.

For the moment she focused on the foreign feeling that spread over her heart, trying to recognize it. She could have sat on that stone bench all day with Henry beside her. The feeling pumped and pounded and grew, reaching to every inch of her skin until she could have no doubt over what it was. Hope. Happiness. Maybe even the possibility of love.

Chapter 11

"Have you found yer wife some ladies to converse with yet?" Silas asked after swallowing a swig of water.

Henry had spent the early morning practicing his fencing with Silas yet again, besting him in each match, fueled by the hope that had begun to burn inside him. He smiled. "No, I tried and failed horribly. Mrs. Morton and her daughters had nothing but disdainful remarks to give. I suppose Eleanor will just have to spend more time with me." Henry was not at all opposed to such a thing. They had spent most of their days together since that morning in the gardens, and he could easily envision many days just like it. Arthur was growing increasingly comfortable in his company too, and Henry adored the boy.

He planned to find Eleanor as soon as he finished fencing, in the hopes that they could take the ride they had yet to take.

"You aren't falling in love with her are ye?"

Henry raised his eyebrows at the bold question from his valet but couldn't help but smile. "What is wrong with falling in love with my own wife?"

"Well, that didn't answer my question." Silas combed a hand through his ginger hair, resting his elbow against the wall.

Because he liked to irk Silas, Henry held his tongue, keeping the answer to himself. His feelings for Eleanor were altogether confusing, and he didn't care to explain it all to Silas. He had never imagined that she would have the effect on him that she did, that she would give him so many reasons to smile, or that his heart would stall when she walked into a room. He had been hiding the answer from himself, afraid of acknowledging it.

Henry had not entered into this marriage with any expectation of love, and neither had Eleanor. It was *possible* that he would fall in love with her. But what if, in her sight, he remained a simple guardian-figure or a friend? The thought stung, so he pushed it away.

"Are you not going to tell me?" Silas gasped, pressing his hand to his chest. He waved a finger at Henry. "You needn't tell me. I already know the answer."

Henry bit the inside of his cheek, picking up a towel and exiting the room. Silas's laughter followed him down the hall until the door swung shut.

Eleanor had never seen so many books in one place. She had decided to explore the library in more detail, hoping to find stories to read to Arthur. Over the past several days, she and Henry had met in the library with Arthur in the mornings, beginning to teach him the basics of mathematics, reading, and geography.

Eleanor was learning new things about Henry every day. She had not known that Henry had a desire to travel. He spoke of all that he had learned about India, France, and Africa through his readings. The passage of time came unnoticed when she was with Henry, and Arthur quite enjoyed learning from him. Eleanor learned much from him as well, things she had never been taught in her youth.

Eleanor had done all she could to teach Arthur when they lived in the North, but her own education had not been as thorough as she would have liked it to be, and without books to teach him from, he grew bored quite easily. She would never grow bored in Henry's company, and neither would Arthur. When discussing a topic he was passionate about, Henry's eyes grew wide, his voice deep with conviction. She found herself fascinated by his words.

The dinner party at Pengrave was just a week away. While she was excited to see Adam, she found that she was not as impatient as she had been when his letter first arrived. She was quite comfortable here in her new home. Her old worries had begun to feel distant and untouchable. It was as if she were growing a pair of wings, set on taking her to new heights, new destinations, and giving her the strength to fly.

And she owed it all to Henry.

In her previous experience, a husband was a man to fear, to submit to, to be controlled by. Henry contradicted that in every way. Of all the things he had been teaching her, that was the most important lesson of all.

She had never thought it possible to fall in love with her husband. The feeling was so new that she didn't yet know what to call it. The expectation that had been set with their marriage at the beginning was that of a necessary arrangement. She had never expected to care so deeply for Henry. What if Henry did not care for her the way she had begun to care for him? He had told her that he cared for her, and she knew he did, but was it simply as a friend? An associate? At times it seemed that she was just something for him to protect, to watch over. Could his affection run deeper than that?

It terrified her. She did not enjoy feeling so vulnerable. She had loved Mr. Quinton once, only to discover that his feelings were not the same. Not in the slightest.

She perused the nearest bookshelf, knowing Arthur to be waiting for her outside. She had left him for just a moment in the gardens. Henry had business to attend to in his study that morning, and she had planned to meet Arthur outside where he would play and explore while she read.

After selecting a book on botany, Eleanor made her way to the back door and outside into the warm summer air. She pulled her bonnet strings tighter, tipping the brim to better shade her face from the sun. With determined strides, she went straight to the gardens where she had left Arthur near their favorite yellow rose bush. As she rounded the stone path, she found the area deserted.

"Arthur?" Her heart pounded. "Please do not hide from me."

She hurried forward, peering behind the bush. He was not there.

"Arthur!" she called, checking behind the bench and behind the nearby shrubs. Her pulse quickened and her legs began shaking. Where could he have gone? She had told him to stay by the rose bush until she returned outside, and he never disobeyed her. Could he have gone farther out on the lawn to explore? As uncharacteristic as it seemed, it was certainly still a possibility.

She carried herself into a run, threading through the gardens and back out to the more open area of the lawn. The stables were on the east side, followed by a copse of trees and a large hill that led to the path into town. She scanned the area, her breath quickening with fear. "Arthur!"

A faint voice met her ears from the distance. "Mama!"

"Arthur?" She ran toward the sound, unease settling in her stomach. The tone of Arthur's voice was one of fear, and she had heard the tears behind it.

"Mama!" he called again, sobbing. The sound was closer now as she ran across the lawn toward the trees. She glanced around frantically, searching for any sight of him.

"Arthur, where are you?" She glanced upward when she heard the rustling of leaves. Arthur sat on a branch, far up in a tree, hugging the trunk. Tears streamed down his face, his cheeks splotched with red, his blue eyes round with terror.

Eleanor pressed her hands against the bark of the trunk. "Arthur! What are you doing up there?" She had never known him to dare something as adventurous as climbing a tree. She had only left him in the gardens for a few short minutes. She noticed the scrapes on his arms. He seemed to have been in a great hurry to climb the tree.

She measured the distance with her gaze. He was so high up. She couldn't possibly reach him unless she climbed the tree too.

"I need you to try to come down," she said, reaching her arms up as high as she could. "Come down to that branch there." She pointed at the one just above her arms. "I will lift you down."

Arthur shook his head, clinging to the trunk so tightly his arms trembled.

She stepped back, taking a deep breath. "You must be brave, Arthur. Please try."

"No." He shook his head, fat tears continuing their fall down his cheeks. He sniffed, his words barely comprehensible. "Grandpapa w-will come and get me if I—I don't stay up here."

Eleanor's stomach contracted with dread. "What?"

"Grandpapa will find me."

Shivers tingled the back of Eleanor's neck, and she jerked her gaze behind her. What could have made Arthur afraid of the elder Mr. Quinton on a day like today? "Grandpapa is not here."

"Yes, he is." Arthur removed one arm from the tree to rub his nose. "He saw me in the garden, and I ran away."

Eleanor's heart beat so hard it hurt, pounding against her ribs. Her skin grew cold. It couldn't be true. Surely Arthur had been imagining it. "Did he follow you to the tree?" she asked. She couldn't help but make her voice quiet for fear of being overheard by Mr. Quinton. She glanced behind her again. He was not here. He couldn't be.

"No." Arthur took a shaky breath, his sobs subsiding slightly.

"He was not really here. You must have had a nightmare." She said it more for herself than for him, trying to calm her racing heart. Still, her gaze darted in every direction. She saw no sign of the elder Mr. Quinton.

Arthur remained silent, hugging the tree with both arms again.

"You must try to come down."

He shook his head.

Frustration rose inside her. She couldn't leave Arthur

there while she searched for someone to help them, especially not after he had claimed to have seen Mr. Quinton. As implausible as the statement was, she could not help but fear it. What if it were true? What else could have frightened Arthur enough to hide in a tree?

She paced in front of the wide trunk, considering her own ability to climb it. Perhaps if she could make it to the branch she had instructed Arthur to step down to, then she could lift him down to it, climb back down herself, then lift him to the ground from there. She was fairly certain of her ability to get to that first branch, and she had worn her lightest morning gown, the skirt full enough to allow for climbing, as well as her sturdy half boots.

"Very well. I am coming up to help you."

She jumped and grabbed hold of the nearest branch, securing her foot on a knot in the trunk. The mottled bark dug into her palms as she pulled herself up, scraping the front of her dress in the process. She balanced on the branch, sitting as if on a side saddle.

Arthur's feet dangled just above her.

She gathered her breath and her balance, tipping her head up to look at him through the leaves. "Come now, Arthur, take hold of my arm and climb down here." She struggled to balance with one arm outstretched above her. Arthur looked down, his brow pinching, shaking his head again.

"Do not be afraid. I will help you. You can do it." She reached a little higher, but he still refused to take her hand.

Exasperation boiled up inside her. What else could she do?

"What is happening here?" Henry's voice came from below, part amusement, part concern.

Eleanor glanced over her shoulder. Henry stood just

beneath her branch, staring up at her with a bewildered expression.

"Arthur climbed up here and I cannot get him down." She hadn't meant to sound so frustrated, but she could not help it. Coupled with the dread and fear that Arthur had placed in her with his mention of Mr. Quinton, she couldn't think clearly.

Henry walked forward, turning his gaze up to Arthur. "Step down to the branch below you. Your mother will help you onto her lap, and I will lift you down."

Arthur's expression seemed to calm, his arms loosening around the trunk. "But it is too far away."

"I think you must be a very strong boy if you climbed up there all by yourself. It should not be so very hard to climb down. That is the easy part." Henry smiled, clearing the tension in the air with the gentle calmness of his voice. "Do not look at the ground, just look at me, or look at your mother."

Arthur looked at the ground anyway.

His arms tightened around the tree again.

Henry sighed, reaching his arms up toward Eleanor. Before she knew what he was doing, he had a firm grip on her waist. Realizing he intended to help her down, she gripped his upper arms. He lifted her with little effort, placing her gently on the ground in front of him. His hands lingered on her waist for a brief moment, his face very near to her own. His eyes bore into hers, and she had to look away, her heart leaping from a combination of exhilaration, fear, and sudden longing. Her gaze landed on his smiling lips, which did similar things to her already pounding heart.

"I never thought I would see you attempt to scale a tree," he said, the amusement returning to his voice.

She could think of little else besides the way his hands felt, strong and warm through the fabric of her dress, and the way his lips quirked to one side as he spoke. She lifted her gaze back to his eyes. She was both relieved and disappointed when he stepped away, turning his attention to the tree.

Henry took hold of the same branch she had been sitting on, hoisting himself up with much less effort than it had taken her. He reached upward, beckoning Arthur with his hand. "Come. There is no need to be afraid."

To Eleanor's surprise, Arthur let go of the trunk, leaning forward with both arms outstretched. Henry grunted as his balance faltered, catching himself on the trunk before pulling Arthur into his arms.

Henry handed Arthur down to Eleanor before alighting from the branch, landing heavily on the grass. Arthur clung to Eleanor, his arms wrapped around her neck and shoulders almost as tightly as he had held to the trunk of the tree. His face was buried in her sleeve.

Henry brushed bits of bark from his trousers before meeting Eleanor's eyes with concern. "What compelled him to climb up there?"

Her gaze darted around them again, surveying every direction. "He thought he saw Mr. Quinton on the property." Even as she said the words, her chest tightened with dread.

Henry frowned, taking a step closer to them. "Your late husband's father? How could he have discovered your location?"

"I am certain Arthur imagined it. I do not see how Mr. Quinton could have found us." She shook her head fast, unwilling to believe that they had been discovered.

Henry touched her shoulder with reassurance. "There

is nothing he can do to take Arthur. The courts will be on our side if he tries to regain custody. We have Edward to vouch for us, and it seems the Marquess of Seaford is a close friend of your brother's. We have connections that outrank Mr. Quinton's and influence that he will never have."

She exhaled a long breath. "You are right, but it is still troubling."

"Yes." Henry rubbed his chin, glancing behind him. "I will inform my servants to keep a careful watch on the grounds and to direct any unwelcome visitors to the front doors."

Would it be enough? Eleanor chewed her lower lip. "Arthur," she said, keeping her voice soft. He lifted his head from her shoulder, his eyes puffy. "Where did you see Grandpapa? Did he speak to you?"

He nodded. "He was by the yellow flowers. He said he wanted to take me home. I ran away."

Eleanor exchanged a glance with Henry. "Are you certain it was him?" Henry asked.

Arthur nodded again, his chin beginning to quiver. "I don't want to go with him, Mama. I want to stay here."

"I know," she whispered.

"You will not go anywhere with Mr. Quinton." Henry stepped forward, brushing Arthur's hair back from his forehead. Arthur stared up at Henry, desperation in his gaze. Eleanor watched as Arthur's expression slowly relaxed.

"You are safe here. I promise."

Eleanor held tightly to the promise. That had been the purpose for this marriage, to protect Arthur from Mr. Quinton.

Had he found them already?

Chapter 12

As the days passed, Arthur's description of Mr. Quinton on the property became less and less plausible. Henry had instructed all his servants to inform him of any sight of a stranger near their property, and thus far, there had been no sight of him.

If Mr. Quinton knew of Eleanor and Arthur's location, Henry could think of no reason why he would not call upon them to visit his grandson and discuss his desire for custody. Why would he sneak around the property without making himself known?

He wanted to speak to Arthur with more detail on the matter, but he didn't wish to scare the boy when he was finally growing comfortable around him, so he strived to keep his time spent with Eleanor and Arthur light, happy, and free of worry.

One morning when he ventured down to the breakfast room, he found Arthur with Adeline, his nursemaid, where she was helping him arrange a plate of food.

Adeline glanced up when Henry entered, greeting him with her usual curtsy and smile. She was a quiet sort, much like Arthur. Henry supposed that was why they got along so well.

Henry smiled down at him. "Good morning, Arthur."

"Good morning."

"Where is your mother?"

"She is still sleeping." Arthur turned his gaze to the fruit tray, pointing timidly at a slice of orange. Adeline served it onto his plate, taking it to the table and helping Arthur onto the tall chair. Adeline glanced at Henry as she pushed Arthur's chair closer to the table. "The mistress was up with Arthur much in the night. He has nightmares, you see. I suspect she is very tired."

Henry leaned against the wall. He could think of many reasons why Arthur might have nightmares, and all of them had to do with his previous home and the Quinton men. Adeline did not know what Arthur had been through there. Determination grew within him to be a positive influence in Arthur's life.

Henry needed to give him a distraction from his troubled thoughts. Perhaps then he would not have so many nightmares.

He sat down at the table beside Arthur, who glanced over at him as he took a bite of bread.

"Have you ever played with a bilbocatch before, Arthur?"

The boy shook his head, his cheeks full. He swallowed. "What's a bilfocash?"

"Bilbocatch," Henry corrected, smiling. "It is a toy that I loved when I was a child, and I have one, just for you. It is a wooden rod with a handle, that has a ball attached to a string. Would you like to play when you have finished eating?"

A gleam of excitement entered Arthur's eyes, and he nodded, scooping up his food with greater speed. Henry fetched two bilbocatches and returned to the breakfast room. When Arthur saw the toy, he finished his plate within minutes and slid down from his chair without Adeline's assistance.

Henry extended his hand and Arthur took it, walking along beside him until they found a place on the lawn. Henry handed one of the bilbocatches to Arthur, who stared at it in awe. He held it as if it were a mysterious object, dangerous even. He had no idea of what he was supposed to do with it.

Henry's heart stung to see that Arthur had never played with one before. It had been Henry's favorite pastime as a young boy, always creating competitions with Edward as to who could catch their ball in the cup consecutively for the longest.

"You must grip it there," Henry pointed at the handle.

Arthur adjusted his fingers to the correct place, glancing up at Henry for approval.

"That is perfect. Now, see the ball that hangs from the string? You must thrust the cup into the air so the ball flies upward, then try to catch it on the cup."

Arthur's brow scrunched in confusion, so Henry demonstrated. He stood with his arm in front of him, holding the handle just below the cup. The ball swung gently, and he waited until it was perfectly still. In one motion, he flicked the cup upward, sending the ball swinging in the air. He repositioned the small cup below it and caught the ball.

Arthur smiled, a small giggle escaping him. He extended his arm as Henry had, waiting for further instruction. His first few attempts he failed to catch the ball, but after a minute or two, he managed to catch it for a brief moment before it fell off again.

"See, it is not so difficult." Henry smiled, patting him on the back. Arthur's grin had doubled in size since his first attempt, and he continued to swing the ball.

Amid the clattering of the bilbocatches, Henry hadn't heard the rushed footsteps behind him.

"Arthur!" Eleanor's voice was unmistakable as she turned the corner that led to Henry's and Arthur's location near the gardens.

Henry turned around, surprised to see the concern on her face. The moment she saw him, her posture slackened, her brow smoothing over. "Oh. I thought—" she stopped, biting her lower lip. "I did not know where Arthur was." She pressed her hand against her side, breathing heavily. "I was worried something had—had happened to him." Her voice still trembled, from exertion or worry, he couldn't tell. He was glad to see that she was relieved when she saw Arthur with him but wished that she did not have to live in such fear.

"I should have told you I had him with me," Henry said. "I wanted to let you rest."

Her eyes flicked to the bilbocatches, as if noticing them for the first time. Her expression lightened, a smile stealing across her face. "I have not seen one of those since I was a child."

Henry extended his toward her. "Would you like to join us?"

She met his eyes, reservation in her gaze. "Me?"

"Yes, you."

She took the bilbocatch gently, holding it in a manner quite similar to Arthur. "I'm not certain I remember how to play." She laughed quietly, studying every angle of the toy as if it were a specimen meant for scientific study.

He chuckled, noticing her grip was in the same place Arthur's had been, her hand wrapped around the cup. He moved forward until he stood beside her, carefully taking hold of the base of the bilbocatch, then taking her wrist in his other hand, sliding his fingers over hers. Every time he touched her, he was surprised by the effect it had on him. It never failed to set his pulse moving a little faster.

His stomach flipped when her eyes met his. They were so blue. He returned his gaze to their hands, using his fingers to shift hers downward.

"There," he said, taking a breath. "Hold it just there." He had trouble breathing in that moment, with all the scents of her, the smell of roses wafting up from her clothing. He took a step back.

She stared intently at her bilbocatch. "And now do I swing the ball and try to catch it on the cup?"

"Yes." Henry's voice had turned far too professional, as if he were instructing a pupil. He was instructing her, yes, but she was far more than his pupil. He cleared his throat.

Eleanor gave it her best swing, catching the ball perfectly on top of the cup. She turned to him in triumph, her smile wide and bright. "Oh! Look!"

He laughed, warmth spreading through his chest at the image of pure delight on her face. She turned to Arthur, showing him the result of her first attempt as well. He grinned up at her, giggling as he tried again, showing no signs of discouragement as his ball missed the cup over and over again. Henry decided that he ought to introduce Arthur to spillikins and paper ships before he grew too old to appreciate them. Henry, of course, would always appreciate such games, and it seemed Eleanor would too.

For several minutes, Henry watched as Eleanor and Arthur practiced bilbocatch, laughing and smiling like he had never seen before. He would do anything to keep them so content. His own smile grew with each passing minute. Eleanor eventually set her bilbocatch down on the grass, letting out a long, contented sigh. She turned to Henry, the dark curls on her forehead twisting slightly in the breeze. "Arthur seems to love it," she said, walking across the grass.

Henry sat down beneath the nearest tree, and Eleanor joined him. They watched, laughing as Arthur spun in a circle, trying to catch the ball at the same time.

"He does. I should have brought out the toy sooner."

He glanced at Eleanor, surprised to see a sheen of moisture on her eyes, though her mouth still smiled. "I have never seen him so free or heard him laugh so much."

Henry watched Arthur, deep affection and pride glowing within him. Arthur was not his son by birth, but he was his stepson. He had only known him for a matter of weeks, and yet the pride he felt for him was stronger than what he ever could have imagined he would feel for a son.

"You remind me of my mother," Henry said.

Eleanor eyed him, silently awaiting his explanation.

"You truly care about your son, and you have taught him well. You are strong, loyal, and fiercely protective. He knows he can rely on you. If there is anything that should exist between mother and child it is trust and love. You and Arthur have both, just as I had with my mother."

Eleanor rubbed her fingers through the grass, plucking out blades one at a time. Her smile had slackened, and deep thought showed in her profile. "I believe that is true for any other relationship as well. Trust is vital."

"And love?" Henry waited for her eyes to meet his, to see if he could decipher anything from them. He certainly couldn't by her actions. Did she care for him as deeply as he was coming to care for her? He believed that she was beginning to trust him, but he wanted more than that.

Grace had told him that love was a choice, but when it came to Eleanor, he was losing all choice in the matter. He couldn't help but fall in love with her. His choice had been taken away when he first saw her smile and heard her laugh. His heart had surrendered.

But Eleanor had been hurt by love, tortured by it, and had learned not to trust when a man told her he loved her. How could he expect her to believe him if he did? He did not want to ruin the friendship they were building—he did not want to ruin the trust he had worked so hard for by scaring her away.

Eleanor glanced up at him, her cheeks growing pink at the centers as they often did. That must have meant something, didn't it? Eleanor was difficult to read. He still felt a distance between them, a gap he did not know how to bridge.

"Love is very important too." Eleanor said, her voice soft and thoughtful. "I think love is not possible without trust. But when trust is betrayed, love begins to hurt and destroy the person that dared to love at all. Thus, love betrays that person too." There was passion behind her words. Her voice was strong, but a tremor could still be heard behind it. Eleanor began picking at the grass again, her shoulders square, her chin firm.

Henry leaned closer, trying to draw her gaze back to his face. "Do you not think love can also heal?"

Eleanor's posture softened, and she looked up at him.

She was silent for a long moment before answering, searching his eyes. "Yes."

"But only if you dare to trust first. And only if you let yourself be healed."

Her jaw tightened, her eyes settling on his with a weight he had never seen before. She looked as if she were about to speak, her brows drawing together and her lips parting.

Before she could say a word, Arthur ran across the grass, his giggles calling both their gazes.

"Look!" He held up the bilbocatch, the ball resting neatly on top.

Henry smiled, beckoning Arthur closer with his hand. "I knew you would be very skilled with a bilbocatch." Henry winked.

Arthur beamed with pride, settling down on the grass beside them. "I wike it," he said, studying the ball, rolling it between his hands.

Eleanor laughed, leaning forward to ruffle his hair. "I think you love it."

He nodded, looking up at Henry from under his lashes.

Henry chuckled, leaning back on his hands. His right hand settled in the grass directly beside Eleanor's hand, his index finger touching hers in the grass. He saw her arm tighten, but she didn't move, and her posture slowly relaxed. He adjusted his arm, his elbow brushing against hers.

"I am glad you like your new toy. Do you enjoy the rocking horse in your room as well?" Henry asked Arthur.

He nodded, just a small motion. "Very much."

"When you are bigger, I will teach you to ride a real horse."

Arthur's eyes shone with excitement, and he turned his gaze to the stables. "A real horse?"

"Of course. You will be a very skilled rider, I am certain

of it." He nudged Eleanor. "I believe your mother still owes me a ride."

Eleanor's lips twisted into a grin. They had been meaning to take a ride every morning, but she had either been sleeping late after staying up so long with Arthur, or he had been busy in his study.

Henry turned his gaze back to Arthur. "Is there anything else you would like to have in your new home?"

Arthur looked up at the sky, as if he were deeply pondering the question.

"You may ask for anything you wish," Henry said.

Arthur lay down, picking up a handful of grass just as his mother had. He was silent for a long moment before deciding on his answer. "I want brothers and sisters."

Henry dropped his chin, chuckling. Eleanor tightened, and he glanced at her face. Her cheeks had darkened to a deeper shade of pink. He and Eleanor had never discussed such a thing. When he did not respond, Arthur frowned.

"May I have brothers and sisters?"

Henry raised his eyebrows, not expecting to feel so uncomfortable. He felt his own face growing hot, and he was suddenly afraid to look at Eleanor. Blast it, why was he being such a ninny? "Perhaps…in time, I may—er—we may have brothers and sisters for you." Could he have possibly sounded more pathetically awkward? He took a deep breath, glancing at Eleanor, who had begun plucking blades of grass again.

Fortunately, Arthur seemed to be satisfied with his response, returning his attention to the bilbocatch. Henry did hope to one day grow their family, but he would give Eleanor all the time she needed to trust him, to love him, if she ever could. He would wait forever if it was necessary, and he would never give up on the possibility of a marriage of deep affection and love. He hoped it was possible. His heart pounded when he looked at her, at the pink that had begun fading from her cheeks, the tight pinching of her lips. He felt he was constantly at a battle between wanting to show her how much he cared but being afraid of scaring her away. The slightest touch could frighten her. He wanted to kiss her, to hold her in his arms, but he didn't know if the risk was worth it. But blast it, he *wanted* to kiss her.

Arthur began speaking about his rocking horse, and Henry suggested that he name it. Eleanor listened intently, offering her own suggestions. After much deliberation, the name Charger was decided upon, since the horse was brave enough to charge into battle fearlessly.

They stayed beneath that tree until the afternoon, laughing more often than not, until rain clouds drove them inside. They went to the library to begin Arthur's lessons. Henry began to doubt the wisdom of giving him the bilbocatch, for his lessons were much more distracted with a toy nearby.

Henry found himself distracted as well, but for an entirely different reason. Why must his wife be so enchanting?

The answer to Silas's question from a few days before was perfectly clear.

He had certainly fallen in love with his wife. But trust came first, and he was still not entirely sure she trusted him. And he strongly suspected she still had a secret, one he would have to wait to uncover. As it was, he was not certain he trusted her completely either.

Arthur went to sleep easier that night. There was something different about his eyelids as they fluttered closed, a certain contentedness that Eleanor hadn't seen in a very long time. She stared at him for a long moment, at the roundness of his face, the lashes that swept straight, so long that they bent against his cheeks. She bent over to kiss his forehead, her loose hair falling over his pillow. "Goodnight, little one."

He was already asleep, but she hoped he could feel that she loved him and that he was safe. She blew out the candle beside his bed, taking the other candle into the hallway with her as she made her way back to her own room. The hallway was completely dark aside from the soft halo of light that radiated out from her candlestick.

Henry's door opened. She stopped as she passed the doorway, her heart jumping. She caught herself from dropping the candle, but only just.

"Eleanor," Henry said, his voice lifting in surprise. "I thought you were already asleep. When I saw the light I thought I had left a candle burning in the hallway."

She had never seen Henry without his cravat and waistcoat. He wore his simple white shirt, untucked, his hair slightly mussed. She tried not to think of how shocking her own appearance must have been, with her hair loose, hanging down her back. And she was wearing her night dress, her feet bare on the cold marble floors.

He stared down at her, waiting for her explanation it seemed, but all she could think about at the moment was how it might feel to bury her fingers in his hair, perhaps even contribute to the unruly appearance of it. She swallowed. It struck her as slightly humorous then, that she and Henry had never seen one another so unkept, but nothing about Henry's gaze was humorous as he stared at her with a weight she couldn't explain.

"I was just about to go to sleep, actually. I am sorry to have disturbed you with my light."

Henry's gaze burned through her as he took a step closer, glancing behind her at Arthur's door. "No, do not apologize. I heard that Arthur had a nightmare last night."

She nodded. "Yes, but I believe tonight he will be much better." She avoided Henry's eyes, but she found her attention darting to his lips far more than necessary. What else was there to look at? She had often found his cravat to be a good alternative, but his cravat was regrettably absent this evening.

"If there is anything I may do to help him, please come wake me," Henry's voice was quiet, as if he feared waking Arthur.

"Oh, you need not trouble yourself. I can help him on my own."

Henry shook his head. "You need not do anything on your own any longer."

She was still learning how to accept assistance when she had grown so accustomed to not having it. Henry had already devoted his days to looking after Arthur. He didn't need to devote his nights as well. "Yes, and I thank you for hiring Adeline. She has provided help before."

Henry sighed, a sign of exasperation she hadn't seen before. "That is not what I meant."

A quiet whimper came from Arthur's room, the sound growing slightly before subsiding. Henry fell silent, listening. Eleanor knew it to be a common sound Arthur made in his sleep, and it did not usually signify a nightmare.

"I will ensure he is well," Henry said, taking a stride forward. "You should go to sleep."

"Wait," Eleanor said, her voice hushed. She stopped him, pressing her palm against his chest without thinking.

Henry stopped, his gaze landing on hers with that same weight as before. She found it difficult to pull her hand away. She could feel his heartbeat pulsing through his shirt, thudding against her fingertips.

"There—there is no need for that," she said. "He will be just fine tonight." She started to lower her hand, but Henry caught it, holding it gently in his. She dared a glance at his eyes, and immediately wished she hadn't. Her heart picked up speed. The combination of his closeness, and his touch, and the heat and dim light radiating from the candle was too much. Henry stared at her for a long moment. He released her hand, but the intensity of his gaze did not soften. She felt trapped by it, pulled by it, and it would not let her escape.

"If you are certain," he said finally, the words somewhat forced.

She pressed her lips together, nodding. Henry's attention fell to her lips, and her heart seized. Just as quickly, he returned his gaze to hers. A fleeting thought crossed her mind—she wished he would kiss her. Did he want to? She caught a glimpse of longing in his expression, and she had to stop herself from stepping closer, filling the space between them. She tried to breathe steadily, but it was suddenly very difficult.

When Mr. Quinton had kissed her, she had felt nothing. What would a kiss from Henry feel like? Emotion clawed at her heart, a longing to feel loved. Were Henry's feelings for her the same as her own? Did he wish to kiss her because he cared for her as deeply as she cared for him? She had none of the answers. All she knew was that she was falling, and she lacked the strength to catch herself.

Henry drew a deep breath, taking a large step backward toward the doorway behind him. "Goodnight," he said, his voice somewhat abrupt.

"Goodnight." She stepped back too, bustling far too quickly back to her own room. She closed the door behind her, leaning against the cool wood.

With one puff of air, she blew out her candle.

Chapter 13

Eleanor spent most of the next morning and afternoon with Arthur, reading some of the books she had found in the library. That night, she and Henry would be traveling to Seaford for the dinner party. She would have to leave Arthur at home, so she wanted to spend as much time with him that day as possible.

Seaford was not far, and she knew Adeline would keep Arthur occupied while she and Henry were away. She hoped she could visit Brighton soon with Arthur, to show him more of the town she had grown up in. But for tonight, he would have to stay home. She did not think a four-year-old boy would be welcome at a dinner party at the home of a marquess.

When late afternoon came, her maid helped her get ready for the party. She wore one of the gowns she had selected in Brighton with Amelia, a deep blue with short, layered sleeves, a lace-trimmed neckline, and a matching satin sash. Mary styled her hair in a more elaborate arrangement than usual, piling most of her hair at the crown of her head, leaving a single tendril to circle the back of her neck, resting over her shoulder and bodice.

She could hardly remember the last time such care had been taken with her appearance, and she was struck with melancholy at the thought of the days that were long past, when her mother had combed her hair at night.

When she met Henry in the drawing room to leave, he seemed surprised to see her so well presented. Of course he would be, after her unruly appearance the night before in the hallway.

She took him in with her gaze. His hair had been neatly styled, and he wore a simple grey waistcoat. To her relief, his cravat was tied. At least she could have something to look at that did not send her stomach spiraling, or her heart out of rhythm.

"I am sorry I have been so absent today," Henry said as he walked toward her.

"I understand that you are quite busy." Eleanor smiled. "Please let me know how I may be of assistance in managing the estate."

A small smile curved his lips, his eyes sparking with amusement. "So you are allowed to help me, but I am not allowed to help you?"

She knew he was referring to the night before, when she had insisted on taking care of Arthur on her own, even though she had been exhausted. She looked down at her gloves, smiling. "No, I suppose not."

When she looked up again, he was still smiling, but his voice was softer. "You are beautiful."

Her heart leapt at his words. She had known flattery before, but never flattery so obviously genuine, mingled with a hint of shyness that sent familiar threads of warmth through her heart. His compliment was given depth through his smile, his eyes, and she knew he meant more than the fact that she had worn an elaborate dress and hair style. Henry always saw far deeper than that. "Thank you," she said.

He brushed aside one of her curls. "Remember?" he said, his voice low. "You mustn't thank me for anything, especially for declaring something so obvious."

She couldn't stop her smile from widening. He extended his arm. She took his elbow, wrapping her hand firmly around it.

Adeline brought Arthur into the room to bid them farewell. Upon seeing him, Eleanor felt a sudden pang of guilt for leaving. She had to remind herself that Henry had hired Adeline for a reason. Eleanor needed to do something for herself tonight, and Arthur would be well taken care of. He seemed happy enough to be there with Adeline, holding her hand and smiling up at her.

Eleanor bent down to kiss the top of his head, and Henry ruffled his hair. Her heart warmed at the sight.

"You be good to Adeline while we are away," Eleanor said.

"Oh, I am certain he will be," Adeline said. She rarely spoke, but when she did, her voice seemed to shake, as if she were too shy to even say a few words.

Eleanor stole another glance at Arthur. She had never been apart from him for an evening. It frightened her. She knew the servants to be capable of looking after him, but she was still slightly unsettled leaving him behind.

Arthur's brow creased. "Will you come back soon, Mama?"

"I will be back to give you a kiss before you go to sleep

tonight," Eleanor promised. "Perhaps Adeline will play bilbocatch with you."

Arthur seemed to cheer up at that suggestion, glancing up at the nursemaid. "I wike bilfocash."

Adeline squeezed his hand. "As do I."

Eleanor gave Arthur one more kiss before Henry led her out of the room. She waved in the doorway.

Adeline smiled, waving her own farewell in their direction.

To Eleanor's relief, all the guests at Pengrave were familiar in one way or another. Lord Seaford had been a dear childhood friend of Adam's through their time spent at the same boarding school. Eleanor had not become acquainted with him until that evening, and she found herself wishing she had met him long before that. He and his wife were two of the most friendly, agreeable people she had ever met.

Tall, lanky, with dark curls that spilled over his forehead and an ever-present smile, Lord Seaford was not at all how she had imagined a marquess to be. The title had fallen upon him unexpectedly, she had learned, as well as the estate, so he had not been born to such privilege. His wife, small and red-haired, was slightly quieter, but she teased her husband mercilessly.

"Philip! You mustn't bore our guests with another description of your apple tree."

"How could they be bored? I know for a fact that my horses adore hearing about my apple tree, so I assumed our guests would too."

"The horses do not understand you."

"Perhaps not, but they love to eat the apples, and so will our guests." Lord Seaford winked at his wife before turning to Eleanor and Henry. "I have had a delicious apple tart prepared for dessert this evening."

Eleanor and Henry had been the first guests to arrive, and they sat in the parlor with their host and hostess, awaiting the arrival of Adam, Amelia, and her aunt Margaret. The other guests that would be arriving were Mr. Harrison, his wife, Edward, Grace, and the Baron of Hove, who was Grace's uncle. The prospect of so many guests was daunting, but Eleanor knew she wouldn't receive any scorn from any of them. They knew the truth of her situation, not just the gossip.

So far Eleanor had sensed no disdain from Lord and Lady Seaford, who seemed quite happy to entertain Henry and Eleanor all evening.

Lord Hove was the first of the other guests to arrive. He was a man of average height, with neatly combed grey hair, a yellow waistcoat, and a cane. He offered a flourishing bow when he entered the room, beaming with excitement as Lord and Lady Seaford introduced him to Eleanor and Henry.

"Ah! Mr. Beaumont, it is a pleasure to see you again. Your brother and my niece have always spoken so highly of you."

The baron sat down on the nearby sofa, crossing his leg over his knee. Just moments later, the drawing room door was opened again, and Amelia's aunt Margaret stumbled through it, her cane catching on the edge of the doorframe.

"Oh! Good heavens, I did not mean to make such an entrance," she said around a gasp. Eleanor suspected that more of the woman's inhalations were gasps than not. She straightened her posture, fluffing her greying blonde curls before surveying the room. "Ah, dear Mr. and Mrs. Beaumont. I am very pleased to see you again." She smiled broadly, coming to take a seat beside Eleanor.

"Are you enjoying your time in Brighton?" Eleanor asked.

Margaret nodded, an energetic bounce of her head. "Yes, indeed. It is my favorite place in all of England, as well as its surrounding towns such as Seaford and Worthing, of course." She smiled at their host, her eyes flickering to their other guest, Lord Hove. Eleanor watched with amusement as Margaret's eyes settled on the man. Possessing an obvious inability to hide a single emotion she felt, Margaret's eyes rounded. "Oh, my. He is quite a handsome man, isn't he?"

Eleanor refrained from releasing the laugh that rose in her throat. "Indeed."

Henry seemed to be listening to the conversation as well, for Eleanor heard a small chuckle escape him. "I happen to know that he was widowed years ago," Henry said. "He is quite eligible, I believe."

Margaret's eyes widened.

"Have you yet made his acquaintance?" Eleanor asked.

"No, but I certainly wish to." She winked, and Eleanor's laugh bubbled out.

As if he had heard her request, Lord Seaford beckoned Lord Hove forward to meet Margaret. She stood, leaning heavily on her cane. Eleanor watched their introduction with growing amusement. Lord Hove appeared every bit as smitten with Margaret as she had been with him. The awkwardness of the exchange made her feel slightly better about her first interactions with Henry, although they had certainly been awkward as well.

"Oh my, where did you have your cane polished?" Margaret asked.

"London, I believe." Lord Hove's voice was even more boisterous and friendly than Lord Seaford's. "Yours is quite luminous as well."

"Thank you, sir. I do take great pride in keeping my cane in presentable condition." Margaret's smile was wider than Eleanor had ever seen it, her eyelashes batting in a method that could only be interpreted as flirtatious.

Lord Hove grinned. "As one should. A cane will always be my favorite accessory."

Margaret's smile grew impossibly wider. She did not seem to know what else to say, so she took to staring at his cane again. "I daresay yours is the most fashionable cane I have ever beheld."

Henry nudged Eleanor's arm, and she turned to see him smiling. He tipped his head close to avoid being overheard. "When we grow old, please promise me that we will not speak in endless circles over the attractive qualities of one another's canes."

She stifled her laugh with her gloved fingertips. "Would you prefer a conversation regarding the quality of the physicians that care for our gout or the blacksmith that we pay to pull out our decaying teeth?"

Henry tipped his head back, laughing. "Certainly not."

Eleanor tapped her chin. "Perhaps we might choose to converse on the frustrations that arise due to scratched spectacles or dirty fingerprints on our antique silver. Is that the sort of conversation you would prefer?"

Henry's laughter subsided, his smile softening. "I would prefer a conversation like this."

She grinned, looking into his eyes. She would too. The thought of growing old at Henry's side filled her with so much sudden joy, it shocked her. She could see no other vision for her life now, when just a month ago, she had not even known him. A month ago, she had felt helpless, broken, and her future had been bleak. Now… life was so very different. So very happy.

The sensation of joy only lasted a short moment before reality sneaked into the corners of her mind. She still had not told Henry what had happened that day she left her old life behind. She couldn't bear the thought of him looking at her with caution, or fear, or even disgust. Her heart still hammered at the memory.

Adam and Amelia entered the room, calling her attention to the doorway. She and Henry stood as they walked toward them.

"Eleanor," Adam smiled, clasping her hand between both of his. "I have missed you." She studied his face, sensing a strain behind his smile.

"I have missed you too."

Adam exchanged a glance with Amelia. Did Eleanor see worry in her expression?

"I am glad you were able to come tonight."

"As am I." Eleanor sensed the same worry in Adam's voice that she had seen in Amelia's features. Before she could question what it meant, the rest of the guests arrived, filling the large parlor with the sound of many friendly voices and introductions.

She was seated near Mr. and Mrs. Harrison during the meal. Mr. Harrison's wife, Harriett, was just as amiable as he was. She was Grace's elder sister, but Eleanor never would have guessed it based on either their personalities or their appearances. Harriett spoke with Eleanor with fascination about her gown, jewelry, and hair arrangement, until her husband interrupted with a much more serious topic.

"Have you received any further threats from Mr. Quinton?" The barrister asked, keeping his voice low.

Eleanor glanced at Henry, but he sat across the table, engaged in a conversation with Edward. He did not notice Mr. Harrison's question. She clasped her hands together under the table, trying to ignore the sense of dread that the barrister's question imposed. "No, I have not. I believe he might have given up his efforts to take Arthur." She had been telling herself he had, if only to cope with her fear.

"I hope you are right. At any rate, you are well protected with Mr. Beaumont as your husband."

She nodded, catching Henry's eye from across the table. His brow creased with concern, as he likely noticed the worry that had fallen over her own features.

"You have nothing to worry yourself over, Mrs. Beaumont." Mr. Harrison smiled, the friendly expression putting her at ease, if only for the moment. She was still unsettled by the worry she had seen in Adam. What was he hiding from her?

When the entire meal had been served and the apple tart eaten, Eleanor and the other women removed to the parlor while the men stayed back for their port. She found herself clutching at the fabric of her skirts, impatiently waiting for Henry and Adam to return.

Chapter 14

The ambiance of the dining room was drastically different without the presence of the women. Henry sipped from his cup, eager to return to Eleanor's side. She had appeared worried over something, and he wanted to ensure she was well.

Lord Seaford turned toward Henry, tipping his head to one side with curiosity. "I must admit I do not know the first half of what caused the marriage between yourself and your wife, but I cannot help but suspect a similarity to the circumstances that led me to my wife." He chuckled. "Besides the fact that my wife did not wish to marry me at all."

Henry glanced at Adam. He must have told Lord Seaford at least a small part of the story. "What woman would not wish to marry a marquess?" Henry said, avoiding the question. Eleanor hadn't wanted to marry him either.

"Jane most certainly did not," Lord Seaford said. "I cared for her much more than she cared for me. I still believe it to be true, though she argues to the contrary." He smiled, and Henry found himself experiencing a pang of envy. Would Eleanor ever feel for him what he felt for her? There was still a barrier between them, one he could neither name nor hope to tear down.

With Lord Seaford's laughter, Adam set down his glass, turning to Henry. He had been rather quiet all evening, and still spoke in a low voice. "There is a matter of urgency I must speak with you about."

Henry raised his eyebrows. "What is it?"

"Mr. Quinton sent another letter to my home, addressed to Eleanor. It arrived shortly after she married you. He warned her again to surrender her custody of her son."

Dread pooled in Henry's stomach. He had hoped the man had given up.

"I knew he would not find her, so I responded to the letter simply stating that she never arrived at our residence, and that she was now remarried. He hinted quite clearly in the letter that he still held her in suspicion for her late husband's death. I did not wish to worry Eleanor over it, but I thought you should know."

Henry's mind raced. He had always been curious as to what truly happened to Eleanor's late husband, but he had known the topic to be one that made Eleanor distant. He thought of their conversation, just a few days before. He had told her she had done nothing wrong. A cold sensation settled between his shoulders when he recalled her response.

You have done nothing wrong.

Yes, I have.

He rubbed his forehead, his heart picking up speed. Had Eleanor killed Mr. Quinton? No. He refused to believe it. She was not a murderer. Even if the man had been so cruel as to hurt her, and perhaps he deserved his demise, Henry knew Eleanor could not have deliberately done such a thing. She was too gentle. He knew her character to be more noble than that. Then what had happened?

Adam lowered his voice even further. "Has…Eleanor told you anything else about that day Mr. Quinton died?"

Henry shook his head. "I know nothing."

Adam traced his finger in a circle on the table, his jaw tight, his features focused in deep thought. "Do you think the elder Mr. Quinton's accusations carry any truth?"

Henry's heart pounded, his mind searching for another explanation. Eleanor had run away from the North in such a hurry, and when she had met Henry on her journey, she had lied about her husband still being alive. Had she been afraid of being caught for a crime? He refused to believe it. "I don't know."

The rest of the table had fallen silent, the gazes of Edward, Lord Hove, Mr. Harrison, and Lord Seaford all fixed on Henry and Adam, apparently sensing the tension of the conversation.

For the first time all night, Lord Seaford stopped smiling, his eyes settling on Adam with concern. He didn't pry for information, but simply made a suggestion. "Shall we all rejoin the ladies in the drawing room?"

Adam stood and Henry followed, stepping out the doorway behind the rest of the men. When they entered the hallway, Lord Seaford patted Adam on the shoulder. "You may discuss your matter in privacy."

"Thank you," Adam said, taking a deep breath.

They waited for the rest of the party to disperse before returning to the dining room table.

Adam sat down heavily, running his hand through his dark hair. "I did not want to believe it to be true. I know Mr. Quinton was a terrible man, and after what he did to Eleanor, I might have killed him myself…"

"Agreed," Henry muttered.

"… but how could Eleanor have murdered him?" Adam shook his head. "Still, it seems as though the elder Mr. Quinton's greatest aim is to secure the child and his property for himself, not to have Eleanor punished for the crime."

"We still do not know for certain if a crime was committed," Henry said. "We must learn the truth from Eleanor." He needed to find out. He had done all he could to earn her trust, yet she had still been keeping a secret from him. He did not know what more he could do. "I will find a way to speak with her alone tonight," Henry said. "Perhaps I can convince her to tell me what really happened that day."

Adam stared at him for a long moment. "Are you certain she trusts you enough? Perhaps I should do it."

"She trusts me," Henry said, only partially sure of his words. "She will tell me everything, I assure you."

Adam nodded resolutely. "Very well." He stood, his face grim. "Let us make a plan that allows the two of you to leave the drawing room alone so you may speak with her. I would love to sort this out tonight before you return to Worthing. But if it is true what Mr. Quinton has accused her of, and he has a way to prove it, then she will certainly lose Arthur, and we both will lose her."

Henry's heart seized, the pain surprising him. He could not lose Eleanor, no matter what.

Eleanor craned her neck over the women on the sofa beside her as the men returned to the drawing room. For a moment she thought she saw Henry, but it was only his brother. She waited, watching as each man entered the room, but Henry and Adam were not among them. What had delayed them?

She met Lord Seaford's eyes, who smiled with reassurance as he took a chair beside his wife. "Your husband and brother will be here shortly."

She stared at the door, hoping that *shortly* meant a matter of seconds. Growing up with Adam, she had learned how to decipher his expressions, and she knew how to judge when he was anxious. Tonight, he was certainly anxious about *something*. She glanced at Amelia, who sat near the pianoforte, her own gaze fixed on the door as well. She seemed eager to have Adam arrive as well, but she likely knew what it was that was worrying him. Eleanor was left to wonder.

After several minutes, just when she was tempted to stand up and go in search of them, Henry and Adam entered the room, both their expressions solemn as they looked at her. Her heart thudded. What had happened?

Thankfully, the chair to her right had been left empty. Henry crossed the room and took a seat beside her, throwing her a brief smile. She glanced at Adam, who had stopped in front of Lord Seaford, whispering something to him before sitting down nearby. What were they speaking about? Her curiosity heightened. Is this how Henry felt every time he looked at her?

Lord Seaford smiled when Adam finished his whispering, addressing the room. "Is there anyone that would be willing to venture to the music room upstairs to find my wife's sheet music? I would love to have you hear her latest piece on the violin. She has been practicing with dedication for weeks."

His wife threw him a look of confusion. "Might you send a servant to fetch it? You need not ask one of our guests."

To Eleanor's surprise, Henry stood. "That is not necessary. I will fetch it for you." He looked down at Eleanor. "Would you accompany me?"

She nodded, finding it rather strange, as Lady Seaford had, that they were being sent on such an errand. She stood to take Henry's arm.

"Ah, thank you," Lord Seaford said. "It is the piece on the stand beside the violin. You will not miss it."

Adam's eyes followed them as they walked out into the hall. Eleanor glanced up at Henry as the door closed behind them, silence enfolding the empty hallway. "You have never been to Pengrave, have you? Do you even know the location of the music room?" she asked, raising one eyebrow at him.

Henry shrugged. "I am not entirely certain, but it cannot be very difficult to find." He seemed more nervous than she had ever seen him. What had he and Adam been discussing? They walked quietly down the hall until they reached the staircase. There was something odd in Henry's posture, as if he were anticipating something, thinking deeply over words he hadn't yet spoken. He glanced at her, his eyes heavy, his mouth firm.

"What is the matter?" she asked, unable to contain her curiosity. "You and Adam have been acting rather strangely this evening."

He held onto the banister with one hand as they ascended the staircase, and she trailed slightly behind him, studying his posture. Something was definitely wrong.

He remained silent until they reached the second floor. The level was not as well-lit as the main floor. She could barely make out the features of Henry's face when he stopped walking, tipping his head down to look at her. "I spoke with Adam in the dining room," he said, his voice slow and deliberate.

"What did you speak about?"

Henry sighed, raking a hand over his hair. She had never seen him so uncollected before. "Adam received another letter from Mr. Quinton."

Her heart fell. The hallway seemed to close in around her. "What did the letter say?"

"I did not read it, but Adam said it was essentially a repetition of the same threats he extended before. But with a greater emphasis on his…accusations."

Eleanor could hardly think, hardly breathe. "Did he mention that he knew where I was? That he knew where Arthur was?"

"No. He seemed to believe that you had taken up residence with your brother in Brighton, but the letter was received weeks ago, so he could have discovered your location by now." Henry took a step closer, his eyes boring into hers. "Eleanor. I need you to tell me what truly happened the day you left. I need to know what happened to your late husband. It will not take long for Mr. Quinton to take Arthur if he has a way to prove your guilt."

Eleanor pressed her hand to her stomach, feeling suddenly ill. She closed her eyes. No. She could not speak of that day. She could not tell Henry the truth. She saw the white curtain, the flash of red, all still vivid—too vivid—in her mind.

"Eleanor." Henry's voice broke through her thoughts. "Please tell me." He took her hand, and she realized how violently it shook.

She heard Arthur's scream, so clearly, almost as if it were happening all over again. Tears leaked from her eyes, spilling down over her cheeks. Henry caught them carefully with his thumb, patiently waiting for her to speak.

Her eyes opened, meeting his in the dimness. His hand cupped the side of her face, his eyes pleading. How relieving it would be to confide in him, but how devastating it would be if he knew what she had done, if he recognized the danger she put his reputation in—if he decided he no longer wished to care for her and Arthur. He could very well annul the marriage. She couldn't bear the thought.

He lifted his free hand to the other side of her face, cradling it, his hands gentle, safe, and strong. "Please tell me."

She shook her head, her tears spilling between his fingers. "I cannot tell you."

Henry stared down at her, asking, begging something of her that she didn't understand how to give. There was no uncertainty in truth, but there was too much uncertainty in speaking it in that moment. She had once trusted Mr. Quinton enough to tell him the truth of her dowry, a secret she had been encouraged to keep by her father. Mr. Quinton had used that truth to destroy her. This secret that Henry now demanded of her…what would he do with it? She couldn't bear the thought of losing her and Arthur's new home. She couldn't bear the thought of losing Henry and his good opinion forever.

His voice came again, firmer this time, pleading. "Trust me."

"I don't know how," she said, the words mingled with a sob.

"It is never too late to learn." Henry tipped his head closer. His thumb traced over the corner of her mouth before brushing over her lower lip. She drew a sharp breath before Henry covered her mouth with his. He kissed her the same way he spoke to her and looked at her—carefully, adoringly. He kissed her with all the gentleness and cautious passion she had expected of him. She had never been kissed like that before. She had never been kissed like she was both fragile and strong, wanted and loved. Her heart felt as though it had both broken and healed within seconds, the soft touch of Henry's lips causing a tremor within her, an awakening of the feelings she had been hiding from him and from herself.

He pulled away too soon, pressing his forehead against hers. "I love you, Eleanor." He met her eyes. "I will love you no matter what."

Her legs shook beneath her, her lips burning from Henry's kiss. She knew he was telling her the truth. He did love her. Her heart hammered against her ribs, urging her to answer his question, to tell him all the truths she too had been hiding. She wanted to tell him how much he meant to her, how much she had come to love him, but she couldn't find the words. She could not believe that she had once struggled to say *thank you*. Speaking of love was much more difficult, and speaking of that day she left the North was proving to be the most difficult of all.

He did not ask the question again, but she saw it in his eyes. He wanted to know what happened the day she and Arthur escaped.

For the first time in weeks, she allowed herself to remember.

"I told you that Mr. Quinton had no qualms about striking me, or hurting me, but he never hurt Arthur," she began, taking a deep breath. She swiped at her cheeks, clearing the last of her tears. "Mr. Quinton died the very day we left Brighton." She took a shaking breath. "And it was my fault. Mr. Quinton had been awake late drinking at the local assembly the night before. Arthur was fascinated by Mr. Quinton's favorite pocket watch. Arthur sneaked into his room early the next morning, seeing that his father was still asleep, and took the watch." Eleanor looked away from Henry's face, afraid to see his reaction.

"I—I did not see Arthur in time to stop him. He accidentally broke the watch as he was playing with it. I came out to the hallway just as Mr. Quinton discovered Arthur outside his room with the broken watch. He was furious." She shook her head as a tear escaped. "*Furious.* I have never seen Arthur so frightened. *I* had never been so frightened. But then Mr. Quinton returned to his room, and he brought out his pistol." She swallowed. "He was not in his right mind. He—he aimed it at Arthur and I pushed him." Her tears began anew. "I—I pushed Mr. Quinton as hard as I could, and he fell back. The staircase was behind him, and the pistol fired as he hit the ground. He tumbled down the stairs and I knew," she sniffed, wiping her cheek, "I knew he was dead. I covered him with a white sheet so Arthur would not see, then I packed our things as quickly as I could and ran. I did not want the elder Mr. Quinton to find us. I did not know what else to do."

Henry caught the next tear that fell, and the next, before pulling her into his arms. She rested her head against his chest, both relieved and shocked that he had not pushed her away.

"You saved Arthur's life. That is nothing to be ashamed of," Henry said. "You should have told me sooner."

"I am not ashamed. I was just so afraid." She had no other explanation than that. But she did not want to be afraid any longer. She did not need to be afraid ever again, not with Henry by her side.

"You did the only thing you could have done," he whispered into her hair.

He held her until she stopped shaking, rubbing circles over her back. She would have stayed there forever, but Lord Seaford was likely seconds away from sending someone else to find his music. "Do you think Mr. Quinton will find us?" Eleanor asked, tipping her head up to look at Henry.

His eyes flashed with uncertainty. "I don't know."

"I cannot seem to forget that day Arthur climbed the tree." Her voice was just a whisper, and it sent chills running up and down her own spine.

Henry stared at her for a long moment. "You do not need to worry. There is nothing Mr. Quinton can do to take custody of Arthur. He is helpless. He has no way to prove you were involved in his son's death. It was accidental. With my brother and Lord Seaford to testify to your character, Mr. Quinton will have no chance with the courts." He brushed her hair back, giving her a soft smile. "Not to worry."

She closed her eyes, allowing herself to relax. He was right. She had nothing to worry about.

They found the music room without any trouble, taking the music from the stand near the violin as Lord Seaford had instructed. They returned to the party, the last of Eleanor's tears dried. To excuse their extended absence, they claimed that the music room had been much more difficult to find than it actually had been.

Eleanor's cheeks had refused to cool since Henry had

kissed her and told her he loved her. Why had she been too afraid to say it back? She was tired, *tired* of being afraid. But she had told him the truth. Her courage was coming in small pieces, and she had to be grateful for that. The moment she felt courageous again, she would tell Henry how much she loved him. However, she was not feeling courageous at the moment. The only thing she could feel was anxiety. Arthur was so far away.

After speaking of the elder Mr. Quinton again, her feeling of peace had been fleeting. All she could think of was Arthur, and how she could hardly wait to return home to him. She had promised to see him before he went to bed, and it was growing late.

After listening to a poetry reading by Margaret and a violin performance by Lady Seaford, Henry stood, thanking the host and hostess, and excusing them from the party. It seemed he was as eager to return home as she was.

Before they could leave, Adam met them in the hall. Henry explained everything to him, exactly as Eleanor had said it, detailing the events of the day she and Arthur left. Adam hugged her, relaying similar words as Henry had, words meant to reassure her that Mr. Quinton was not a threat to be concerned about. But neither Adam nor Henry had met him. They had not seen the hardness in his eyes, the fierce ownership he had taken over Arthur—as if he had more of right to guardianship than his own mother.

Though Adam expressed the same phrase to Eleanor as Henry had, *not to worry*, her unease only seemed to grow as they took their leave and began the lengthy drive back to Worthing.

Chapter 15

The house was fairly dark when the coach pulled up the drive, very few candles burning in the windows. Henry helped Eleanor down to the ground, keeping her hand in his as they walked toward the front doors. He felt closer to Eleanor than he ever had, now that he knew she trusted him fully. He still did not know if she loved him, but he would wait patiently to find out. He had taken a great deal of time and effort to gain her trust, and he suspected her love was even more difficult to win.

Even so, Henry could think of hardly anything but their kiss as she looked up at him, her eyes shining dark under the night sky, her crimson lips pressing together. She had welcomed it, hadn't she? He could not recall much from the kiss they had shared—nothing except the fact that it had felt nothing short of perfect. He had known that he loved her, but he had not known how madly he loved her until that moment.

He held her hand tightly as they walked through the front doors.

"Do you think Arthur has already gone to bed?" Eleanor asked, glancing toward the staircase.

"I should hope not." Henry followed her gaze up the stairs. "You did promise him a kiss." Henry found himself wishing *he* had received such a promise.

"I do not want to wake him, but I want him to know we are home." Her voice came off nervous.

"Let us see if he is awake," Henry said before leading her up the stairs. The second floor was not as bright as the main level, just as it had been at Pengrave that evening. All the doors in the hallway were closed, not a single candle burning on the wall sconces. Henry found it rather odd that Arthur had been put to bed so early, and Eleanor seemed to have the same thought, her brows pulling together as they walked closer to Arthur's closed door.

Eleanor grabbed the handle, opening it just a crack. Moonlight from his window spilled into the hallway, and she pulled the door open wider before walking into the room. Henry followed, his heart dropping when Eleanor turned to him, her eyes round with concern.

"Arthur is not in bed."

"He isn't?" Henry took two large strides around her, his gaze landing on the made bed, with no sign that Arthur had been in it that night. His chest constricted with dread. "Perhaps he is with Adeline in the library. He does enjoy stories before bed."

Eleanor seemed to relax slightly at his suggestion. "Yes, that could be so."

Henry led the way out of the room and down the stairs. When they reached the library, his dread intensified. The doors were closed, with no sign of light within. Henry walked inside, finding the interior of the room deserted.

"Henry," Eleanor's voice cracked as she paced the hall. "Where else could he be?"

He stopped her, taking her hands in his to calm their shaking. "Not to worry. He must be with Adeline somewhere. We must first find her, and then we will have found Arthur."

Eleanor nodded. "They could be in the kitchen? I know your cook has given Arthur scraps of dough during her evening baking. Perhaps he wandered there."

"That is very plausible," Henry said, trying to keep his voice positive. His own chest still felt weighed down by worry. *Nothing has happened to Arthur*, he tried to reassure himself. He couldn't imagine Adeline leaving Arthur's side for long enough for him to get lost. But where the devil was she?

The kitchen was also empty. Eleanor framed her face with her hands, taking a deep breath. "I knew we should not have left him."

Henry hated to see Eleanor like this. She began walking down the hall, stopping at every door and peering through it.

"Arthur!" she called. "Where are you?"

"Let us check below stairs. Adeline might have taken him down with the other servants." Henry could not imagine why she would do that, but it was still a possibility. They hurried to the main level. Henry started toward the servant's doors, but stopped when Silas rounded the corner, carrying a stack of Henry's freshly washed trousers. "Ah, good evening."

"Silas," Henry said. "Would you assist us for a moment? We cannot seem to find Adeline, the nursemaid. Arthur was left in her care."

Silas frowned. "I haven't seen Adeline all evening, sir."

Henry exchanged a glance with Eleanor, who had paled significantly.

"But I've been below stairs," Silas said, shifting the stack of clothing to one arm, scratching his freckled forehead. "I s'pose she could be outside with the boy."

Henry's heart picked up speed, his senses on high alert. Eleanor's face exhibited the same confusion he felt. "I do not understand. Arthur would never run away, and Adeline is perfectly capable of looking after him." She paused, her eyes potent with fear. "Do you think Mr. Quinton came to the property?"

Henry could not deny that the thought had crossed his mind. He exhaled, running his hand over his hair. His anxiety was beginning to match Eleanor's. "I do not see how he could have found a way past my servants. I instructed them to keep a close watch on the property, and if he had tried to apprehend him, Adeline would have made enough noise to draw attention to him and receive help."

Henry enlisted the assistance of his butler, two stable hands, his groundskeeper, and Silas, all of whom helped circle the house and property in search of Arthur and Adeline. Henry kept Eleanor at his side as they searched, calling Arthur's name. They even checked the same tree he had climbed before, finding the branches empty and dark.

"Look!" Eleanor bent over near the base of the tree.

Arthur's bilbocatch lay half buried in the overgrown grass. Henry picked it up, a cold chill climbing over his shoulders.

"He was here." Eleanor looked up at him, her eyes flashing with the same dread he felt. "It must have been Mr. Quinton. He found us, Henry." She shook her head, covering her mouth. "He took Arthur, and he took Adeline with them."

Henry studied the grass that led to the road beyond the trees. Silas stood nearby, seemingly noticing the same thing Henry did.

"Horse hooves," Silas said.

"Horse hooves, Eleanor," Henry repeated, pointing at the imprints in the grass. "Mr. Quinton must have taken Arthur with him on horseback. If he made his way onto the property from the trees, then he would not have been seen by the servants near the house."

Henry took Eleanor's hand and sprinted to the stables, throwing the doors open with a crash. The horses whinnied in alarm, stamping their hooves in the stalls. Two nearby grooms helped him saddle a horse, and Silas saddled one of his own, intent to help in the search. Henry chose a stallion for Eleanor as well, trusting the horse to be a sedate one. "Are you confident to ride on your own?" he asked her. She had told him that she hadn't ridden in years.

Eleanor nodded, raising her chin. "I will manage."

She appeared so small, so terrified, but trying to be brave. His heart ached. He would find Arthur no matter what it took.

As they led the horses out of the stables, Henry noticed one of his mares was not in her stall. He paused. The doors had not been left open so she could not have wandered out.

He set aside the concern, knowing it to be far less pressing than his current situation.

He helped Eleanor mount first, then mounted beside her. He had set her up with a regular saddle, knowing they could move faster if she rode astride. She still wore the gown she had worn at the party that evening, and thankfully the skirts had enough fullness to situate around the saddle and horse without tearing.

She gripped the reins, her face tightening with determination. Henry mounted his horse and led the way toward the trees. Both Eleanor and Silas helped keep track of the hoof marks in the grass, but as soon as they reached the road, there was no sign of them. They chose to ride east, calling Arthur's name into the darkness. Henry urged his horse faster, galloping over the deserted road. He prayed under his breath. He had promised to keep Eleanor and Arthur safe. He had *promised*, and he was nothing if not a man of his word.

The roads of Worthing were fairly uneven, and when it began to rain, the horses struggled to keep their speed through the mud. They pressed on through the wet storm. He could not wait until the next morning to call on the constable; he had to find Arthur tonight, before his captor took him too far to trace.

Eleanor's voice had gotten stronger, more desperate as she called Arthur's name. They rode as fast as possible. Henry's clothing was soaked all the way through, his vision becoming blurred through the rain that pounded down on his head. The streets were hardly lit, the storm clouds covering the moon.

Henry slowed down to allow Eleanor and Silas to catch up. As lightning struck, his horse shifted anxiously. The sudden light afforded Henry a view of the ground below. His heart jumped in his chest. In front of their own horses was a set of hoof prints, stretching out for as far as he could see. The storm had just begun a few minutes before, so the animal that had made the prints must not have been far ahead.

Henry would wager it had been Mr. Quinton.

At least he was on the right path. He knew an inn to be on this road, and he suspected Mr. Quinton would have stopped there for shelter rather than carry on through the storm. Since the rain could calm at any moment, Henry led the way with more determination, urging his horse faster.

The light of the inn glowed in the distance, and when he finally reached it, he was relieved to see the tracks they had been following stop. He dismounted quickly, leaving his horse with Silas and helping Eleanor down from hers.

"Look who it is," Silas said, walking toward a different horse that had been sheltered nearby.

Henry squinted before realization dawned on him. It was his mare, the one that had been missing from the stables. The coloring of her coat was distinctive, a unique shade of ginger.

"What is she doing here? How could Mr. Quinton have gotten past my stable hands?"

Silas simply shrugged, shaking his head in disbelief.

It was very strange. Henry turned to Eleanor. Her hair had fallen out of its style, hanging wet around her face, splattered in mud, just as it had been that first day he met her on her journey to Brighton. "Do you think Arthur is here?" she asked. Her gaze flickered to the windows of the inn.

"My mare is here, so its rider must be here too." Henry guided her to the front door, pushing it open firmly. Silas followed close behind.

The guests in the parlor glanced up from their plates and card games, shocked by the clatter of the door. The scent of burning pine mingled with wet travelers wafted up to Henry's nose. He could also smell a blend of cinnamon and herbs, as if they had been sprinkled about the room in an attempt to mask the unpleasant smell of the travelers. A man who appeared to be the innkeeper moved from behind the bar to greet them, a look of disapproval and surprise on his face.

Henry met him halfway. "Have you received a young boy with black hair with any of your guests this evening?"

The innkeeper's surprise only seemed to increase with Henry's abrupt question, his bushy grey eyebrows lifting. "I have many guests staying here this evening. I cannot say for certain."

Henry opened his mouth to ask another question but stopped. A dark flash caught his eye near the staircase. He jerked his head toward it, catching sight of a small arm as it rounded the corner to the hall.

He heard Eleanor gasp behind him.

She had seen it too. There were likely a number of children at the inn that night, but he could have sworn it was Arthur he had seen. He stepped away from the innkeeper, rushing toward the hallway with Eleanor close behind.

As he rounded the same corner, he heard a door slam shut near the end of the hall. With large strides, he ran, not caring if he disturbed any slumbering guests.

He stopped in front of the door he thought he had seen closing. Eleanor stopped beside him, her breathing heavy. "Henry, please be careful." Her eyes stared into his, large and round. Her voice fell to a whisper. "Mr. Quinton is dangerous, and I do not know what I would do if he hurt you—or—" she shook her head.

"I will not let him take Arthur," Henry said, his voice gentle and resolute at once. "I promise. Did you see which room he entered?"

She shook her head, leaning toward the nearest door.

"Arthur?" she called.

A small voice met Henry's ears from within the room. "Mama! Ma—" The second half of the word was muffled.

Henry jerked on the handle, but the door was locked. He took two steps back, running at the door with all his strength, aiming his shoulder at it. The door rattled in the frame but did not open. Silas gave it his best try as well, but the door refused to budge.

"What the devil is happening here?" The innkeeper appeared in the hallway, his face red and puffy with anger. His eyes narrowed at Henry. "Get out of my inn at once!"

Eleanor turned to him, desperation in her eyes. "My son has been abducted and he is being held in that room."

The innkeeper's expression immediately shifted to one of concern, and he sprang into action. He withdrew a set of keys from his pocket, muttering to himself as he searched for the correct one. Henry felt close to bursting with impatience as the innkeeper tried three different keys on the door, none of which were correct. After his fifth attempt, the handle turned, and he threw the door open.

Henry barged inside, his gaze jumping around the room. He could see a four-poster bed, a dresser, and a curtained window—no sign of Arthur. When he walked farther into the room, though, he heard a muffled whimper from behind the door.

He stepped around it to see Arthur standing there, a hand firmly covering his mouth—a hand that was much too small to belong to Mr. Quinton.

Henry's gaze jumped up to the woman's face.

It was Adeline.

Chapter 16

Adeline released Arthur as soon as Henry saw her, backing into the corner behind the door.

"Arthur!" Eleanor's voice was a mixture of relief and astonishment.

Henry scooped Arthur up and into his arms, far away from Adeline's reach. Arthur wrapped his arms around Henry's neck, his muscles trembling. Eleanor kissed his cheeks, smoothing her hand over his hair.

Henry turned his gaze back to Adeline, his brow tightening in confusion, his jaw clenching with anger. He couldn't believe she would abduct Arthur, and he couldn't imagine why. But here she was, appearing as guilty as one possibly could, with tears streaming down her face. "What are you doing here with Arthur?" he demanded.

Adeline stepped out from behind the door. She

wrapped her arms around herself, glancing ruefully at him. "I—I'm sorry. I had to take him."

"Why?" From the expression on her face, Henry never would have guessed she would willfully abduct a child.

Adeline sobbed, sniffing loudly. "My master saw your advertisement in town and sent me to take the position of nursemaid at your home. He grew impatient. He w-wanted the boy, and he told me I had to t-take him tonight while you were gone." She took a deep, quaking breath. "I stole your horse. I was instructed to meet him here, but he has not yet arrived. I do not know what he will do to me if he discovered I failed." She wiped her nose. "I am sorry. I am so very sorry. I was so afraid."

Henry glanced at Eleanor, who stared at Adeline with shock. It was not fair how many times Eleanor's trust had been betrayed. Now, after Adeline's betrayal, he knew by some small measure what that felt like. He had trusted Adeline to look after Arthur.

"Mr. Quinton is your master?" Eleanor asked. "You were in his employ before taking the position at our home?"

Adeline nodded. "Yes. He went to Brighton in search of you and Arthur several weeks ago. It did not take long for him to learn of your recent marriage to Mr. Beaumont. Knowing he could no longer secure custody of Arthur through the courts, he decided he needed a different way." She swallowed, looking down shamefully. "He saw the advertisement for your need of a nursemaid, and he sent me to apply. I did not know his plan until he wrote me a letter with detailed instructions and threats, and then he came to the property to speak with me. He tried to take the boy himself, but he was unsuccessful. He needed me to meet him here tonight with Arthur. If I didn't obey he said he'd put my entire family out of work." Her eyes grew round. "I still should not have done it. I should have told you." She continued her sobbing, tears falling down her face and dripping off her chin.

So it had not been Arthur's imagination that day when he climbed the tree—when he claimed to have seen Mr. Quinton. Henry's anger toward Adeline subsided, but was quickly replaced by renewed anger toward Mr. Quinton. Adeline was sixteen years old and he had threatened her, just as he continued to threaten Eleanor. Henry held Arthur tighter in his arms. He needed to get him and Eleanor out of the inn before Mr. Quinton arrived.

The innkeeper watched the exchange with growing concern. "I would never have allowed such a thing to occur at my inn. How atrocious! Where is this man?"

Henry handed Arthur to Eleanor, ushering Silas forward. "If Mr. Quinton is arriving at any moment, we must be prepared outside to meet him."

Eleanor shook her head hard. "No. We must take Arthur home. We must leave before Mr. Quinton finds us."

"I will not risk this happening again," Henry said. "Stay here where you are safe, and Silas and I will wait outside for his arrival."

Eleanor wrapped her arms around Arthur, her face pleading over his shoulder. "Please be careful, Henry."

It was Mr. Quinton who would need to be careful. Henry gritted his teeth, stepping out of the doorway. There was no police force in England that would protect his family for him. It was Henry's duty to do so, to defend their honor and their safety.

Henry turned to Adeline before leaving. "Based on his instructions, do you think Mr. Quinton will be arriving soon?"

She glanced at the clock on the wall and nodded, fear flashing in her eyes. "At any moment."

He would make Mr. Quinton wish he had never dared threaten his family. Henry planned to prove once and for all that he was not born to be a vicar.

※

"Would you like my sword?" Silas asked as they stepped outside the inn.

Henry was not surprised in the slightest that Silas had brought his sword with him. "I do not think it will be necessary," Henry said, squinting through the dark.

They waited for several minutes, Henry's fists clenching at his sides. Where the devil was he? In the distance, a horse came into view, its rider indistinguishable in the dark.

"Is that him?" Silas asked.

As the rider came closer, Henry walked forward a few paces, catching sight of the man's dark hair and large stature. Based on his age and overall appearance, he fit Eleanor's description. The man could only have been Mr. Quinton. Henry's jaw tightened.

Henry watched as the man dismounted and began walking toward the front doors of the inn. Henry and Silas stepped in front of the doors as he approached. The man removed his hat, his hair dripping down his wrinkled skin, two piercing blue eyes meeting Henry's.

"Excuse me, gentlemen." The man's voice was clipped, deep and gruff.

"I'm afraid we cannot let you pass." It took all of Henry's concentration not to plant a facer on the man that very moment, without warning. He took a steadying breath, fixing him with a firm stare instead.

"I beg your pardon?" The man glared at him. "Step aside at once."

"Are you Mr. Quinton?" Henry asked.

The man's eyes flashed with surprise, then suspicion. "Who are you?"

Henry took that as his answer. "I discovered my nursemaid's scheme to deliver my stepson to you here at this inn. I stopped her before she could carry it out." Henry didn't want him to know that Arthur and Eleanor were inside the inn. If he could control it, he wanted to ensure that they never had to see Mr. Quinton again.

The man's eyes hardened, flashing with anger. "Your stepson?"

"I know you have been trespassing on my property, threatening one of my servants, and attempting to abduct Arthur. I will not allow it to continue."

Mr. Quinton's eyes shifted over Henry's shoulder at the inn door behind him before settling on his face again with chilling determination. "I will find a way to take my grandson away from his murderous mother and have her convicted for her crimes."

Henry's anger threatened to spill over. "She has not committed a crime. But you have."

Mr. Quinton paced back a step, laughing quietly under his breath. "Your wife murdered my son before fleeing to Brighton. I will have her stand trial for it, and she will be accused. I cannot stand by while my grandson is in the hands of such a wicked woman."

Henry stepped forward, taking Mr. Quinton by the front of his shirt. He jerked away, pushing Henry against the inn door. Silas intervened, stepping between them.

"Do not utter one more insult against my wife," Henry said.

Mr. Quinton glared at him, his eyes glinting like steel. "Where is the boy?"

"That is none of your concern."

"It most certainly is. If you do not hand him over now, I will have your wife taken to court for her murder of my son."

"She did not murder your son. You have no witnesses to support your claim."

"I am only seeking what is best for the child," Mr. Quinton spat.

"Do you truly claim to care for the boy? You only want control of the properties entitled to him. Did you know your son tried to kill him that day Eleanor fled? The only reason Arthur was safe in that house, living under the care of his own father, was because of Eleanor. She protected him. She saved him."

Mr. Quinton's anger only grew. "My son would never do such a thing."

"Not only did he hurt Arthur that day, but he hurt Eleanor often."

"For reasons she deserved to be punished for."

Henry's jaw clenched, and Silas had to stop him from lunging at Mr. Quinton, pulling Henry back by the shoulders. He took a heavy breath. Henry found himself wishing he did not have such a strong conscience and sense of honor. Being above Mr. Quinton in social status, he could not challenge him to a duel. It would be highly dishonorable. But he was tempted. He assumed Edward would have had no problem thrusting his fist into Mr. Quinton's nose, and he would have encouraged Henry to do it too. Henry had never found himself wishing he was more like Edward.

Henry needed to do *something*. He could not leave Eleanor and Arthur to live in fear any longer. With Mr. Quinton determined to take Arthur, they would never be at peace. His own determination rose, and he squared his shoulders. He could not challenge Mr. Quinton to a duel, but if he could draw a challenge out of Mr. Quinton, then he would readily accept it.

"Your son was a monster of the most despicable sort," Henry said. "He deserved to die that day."

Mr. Quinton's eyes flashed.

"Eleanor did not kill him. His own vile character killed him, his own greed and rage and dishonor." Henry took a step closer to Mr. Quinton, his face just inches away. "And I see quite clearly where he learned it from."

Mr. Quinton growled, slapping Henry across the face with his gloved hand. Henry's cheek stung, but he maintained Mr. Quinton's gaze.

"I challenge you," Mr. Quinton said, his voice shaking with rage. "I challenge you to a duel at dawn tomorrow."

"Until?"

"First blood."

Henry expected nothing less cowardly from a man like Mr. Quinton. "Swords or pistols?"

"Swords."

There was more that needed to be sorted out through the duel than a mere offense of honor. He needed to ensure Mr. Quinton never came near them again. "I wish to set more terms upon this duel. If I am victorious, you will vow never to come near my home or my family again."

"And if I am victorious you will hand over the boy."

"Never."

Mr. Quinton gritted his teeth, his nostrils flaring. Without warning, he reached in his jacket and withdrew a pistol, aiming it at Henry's chest. His heart seized.

The inn door opened behind him, the hinges creaking, momentarily distracting Mr. Quinton. Before the opportunity could pass, Henry grabbed Mr. Quinton's arm, twisting it downward just before his shot cut through the air. A woman's scream came from behind him, and his blood froze. No.

Henry turned around, shocked to see Adeline in the open doorway, crumpled to the ground, clutching her leg. Her skirts were already stained with blood from the wound Mr. Quinton's shot had inflicted. The guests in the parlor all stood, gasping and shouting as men gathered in the doorway to help Adeline.

Eleanor and Arthur stood in the parlor as well, less than three feet behind where Adeline had been standing. Henry met Eleanor's eyes briefly before turning back toward Mr. Quinton. Silas had already torn the pistol from his grip and was struggling to wrestle him to the ground. The innkeeper pushed through the crowd and assisted Silas in detaining Mr. Quinton. They forced him away from the scene, tying his arms behind his back.

Henry stooped over Adeline, taking off his jacket to apply pressure to the wound in her leg. A man claiming to be a surgeon stepped forward to assist Adeline. Her eyes, glossed and filled with tears, met Henry's. "I knew he had a pistol," she choked. "He always carries one. I couldn't let you face him without knowing. I had to come down and warn you."

Henry could hardly believe the man would be so bold as to fire a pistol in front of a crowded inn. The quantity of witnesses was more than enough to send him to court for attempted murder, and it would not be difficult to convict him. Adeline blinked rapidly, cringing in pain.

"Thank you, Adeline," Henry said.

With the surgeon at her side, he stepped away, searching the room for his family.

Henry rushed past the crowd, finding Eleanor and Arthur standing where he had seen them before. He pulled them into his arms. Eleanor held him tightly, her small frame shaking. She rested her head on his chest, and he smoothed his hand over her hair, cradling her head close. She stepped away, and Henry lifted Arthur off the ground. He wrapped his arms around Henry's neck, nestling his head into his shoulder. Arthur likely did not fully understand what had just occurred, but he would never have to see Mr. Quinton again.

"You're safe now," Henry whispered. He wrapped his free arm around Eleanor's shoulders.

She scowled up at him, her features firm. "I thought you were going to die." As soon as she said the words, tears sprung from her eyes. "You cannot do anything so dangerous again, Henry. I forbid it. I cannot lose you."

He stared down at her, surprised by the tenacity of her voice. She seemed surprised by her own words as well, her watery eyes round as they stared up at him. Did she care for him more than he had thought? He couldn't stop hope from rising inside of him. Until she spoke the words, he wouldn't truly know if Eleanor loved him. But for now, as long as Eleanor and Arthur were safe, that was all that mattered.

Chapter 17

Eleanor had never had a sister growing up, but with Amelia and Grace nearby, she felt that she had two very loving, and very insightful sisters. Sisters-in-law at least. She stood on the beach in Brighton near her childhood home, pausing to watch the waves on her walk with Amelia and Grace.

After the events that had occurred two nights before, Henry had suggested that they take a visit to Adam to inform him of what had happened at the inn with Mr. Quinton. Eleanor felt exhausted, both mentally and physically from all that had occurred. Even so, Grace and Amelia had been too cajoling to refuse when they suggested Eleanor take a walk with them to the seaside.

Eleanor quickly discovered the motive behind their suggestion.

"You really must tell him," Amelia said. "You must tell

Henry you love him. It is not as difficult as it may seem. It is three simple words."

That was not true. It was far more than three simple words. Eleanor could not possibly explain to Henry what he meant to her in just three words. "I do not think I can do it," she said, her stomach growing ill just at the thought.

"Yes!" Grace tipped her head back with exasperation. "You must."

"Were you not afraid to tell Edward that you loved him?"

Grace hesitated. "I was not so much afraid than I was uncertain and… rather stubborn. But that was a different situation entirely than your own, and you know Edward and Henry to be two very different sorts of men. Edward would have gone on pursuing me no matter what I said or did, but Henry… he is very patient. He will wait forever to hear those words from you. Would you not choose to put him out of his misery?"

Eleanor's heart pounded. She thought of those years of darkness, when she had feared she would never be loved again—when she had felt so alone, frightened, and filled with despair. She had known love, yes, for she had poured every bit of her love into Arthur, into her family that felt so far away. But she never imagined she could love someone the way she loved Henry, the way she had dreamed of love since she was a young girl. She had given up on it. She had stopped believing in it.

She wanted to clear the uncertainty between herself and Henry. She wanted to share her life with him in every way, with no doubt and fear to come between them. There would be no more secrets, starting with the secret she had been hiding from him and from herself. She loved him.

"How—how do you suggest I... go about telling him? I cannot simply march toward him in the drawing room and declare my feelings." Eleanor gestured up the hill where her childhood home lay.

Grace tapped her chin, a mischievous gleam entering her brown eyes. "Well no, of course not. You must first ensure you are away from any watchful eyes so he may kiss you all he wants when you are finished."

Amelia burst into laughter, covering her mouth with one hand.

Eleanor felt her cheeks grow hot. She had hardly been able to forget the kiss they had shared at the dinner party in Seaford. How *could* one forget something like that?

"I have never known a man as patient as Henry," Grace said. "He will wait for you forever, but if you love him at all, you will not put him through his agony any longer." Grace sighed, touching her hand to her heart. "Oh, Amelia, have you seen the way he looks at her?"

Amelia nodded. "It is so very romantic."

Eleanor had never considered herself to be a romantic, at least not since Mr. Quinton had betrayed her. Even so, she felt a smile pulling ferociously at her lips, a surge of elation entering her heart. Henry had been right about love being capable of healing. Henry was always right.

She turned to the sea, watching the waves as they moved softly with the summer breeze, raising tiny white bubbles as the water spilled over the sand. Courage spilled through her like the water, rushing up and up. "I suppose you are right. I must tell him." She took a deep breath, puffing air out from her cheeks.

Amelia and Grace jumped with excitement, each woman taking one of Eleanor's arms as they walked up the beach. Eleanor's pulse raced as she mulled over the words she was going to say. Could one plan something as important as this? She felt it impossible to put her words together into coherent sentences in her mind. She struggled for air as well as words as they climbed over the rocky bank and up the slope to Adam and Amelia's home.

They found Henry sitting on the back lawn with Arthur and his little cousin Ella, teaching them how to play lawn bowls. He glanced up as they approached, squinting against the sun, his smile widening when he saw Eleanor.

Her heart leapt.

"Come now, Arthur," Grace said, extending her hand. "Shall we go have a cup of water?"

Arthur looked disappointed to be leaving the game, but he obeyed, following Grace, Ella, and Amelia to the back door of the house. Eleanor watched Grace's expression as the door closed, unable to mistake the gleam of mischief in it.

Eleanor took a deep breath and sat down beside Henry. Before she could stop them, her fingers began picking at the grass in front of her. She could feel Henry's gaze on the side of her face. Why did the words refuse to come? She felt as if she had lost the ability to speak. She gathered a small stack of grass on her lap before she found the correct words to begin with. She took a breath, preparing to speak, but Henry spoke first.

"Did you enjoy your walk?" His voice was deep and curious, as it always seemed to be.

She gave a quick nod, meeting his eyes with a smile. "Very much." She looked down again, her eyes settling on the pile of grass on her lap. Perhaps she should count how many blades were there. Yes, that seemed like a wonderful idea. She began counting. *One, two, three, four...*

Henry's gaze burned into the side of her face, unrelenting with each second that passed. He knew she had something to say—why else would Grace and Amelia have whisked the children away with mischievous smiles?

"How long do you wish to stay in Brighton?" Henry asked, breaking the silence once again. "Our stormy horseback ride to the inn was not what I meant when I said I wished to take you on an enjoyable ride through Worthing."

Eleanor laughed, a forced, awkward sound. "That was not an enjoyable ride at all, was it?"

"No, it was not."

She found his eyes again, gathering all the courage she could find within herself. Henry exercised his patience again, keeping his mouth closed until she found the strength to speak.

"I—I have been thinking," Eleanor blurted.

Henry raised his eyebrows with an amused smile. "What have you been thinking about?"

"I have been thinking about the story I used to tell Arthur every night before bed, and the song I used to sing him." She took a breath. "I created that story and that song as a way to dream of the future I wanted." She looked up at Henry, cursing the emotion that choked her again. "My dreams were simple and logical. I wanted to escape the life that I lived. I wanted to give Arthur the freedom to learn and find peace and happiness. That freedom could have come in a number of ways, but in my mind it was as simple as a *light*. A light that would appear in our constant darkness. Something so small and yet so significant."

She looked up at the sky. "I had given up on dreaming of impractical things, like living in a comfortable and beautiful home, or falling in love." She bit her lip as her emotions threatened to overwhelm her. "I never knew I could have everything. I never knew I would find you." A tear slipped down the bridge of her nose. "You are everything I ever wanted, Henry. You have given me everything I ever dreamed of and showed me the things I had forgotten were possible. Kindness, compassion, friendship, love. You are my light, and you are Arthur's light, and I love you." Her voice cracked and she looked at him, tears spilling freely from her eyes now, and she spoke the words again with more conviction. "I love you, Henry."

She breathed, waiting for his response. He stared at her, his gaze all adoration as it swept over her face. He wiped away her tears as he always did, and she sighed.

"I love you, Eleanor," he whispered before looping one arm around her waist, pulling her closer to him on the grass. His mouth broke into a smile as he leaned in, pressing his lips against hers. He kissed her without hesitation, without fear, and she did the same, burying her fingers in his hair. His kisses moved to her cheeks, her forehead, and to her lips again as they sat there on the grass. She wished he would never stop kissing her, and she doubted that he ever would if he had the choice. She had never felt more loved or wanted. Her heart soared, more certain than she had ever been that this was where she belonged—in Henry's arms, by his side, forever.

When the thought struck her that Amelia and Grace might have been watching from the window, Eleanor pulled away, glancing up at the house. Her cheeks grew hot when the drapes snapped closed.

She met Henry's eyes, laughing when she saw the mess she had made of his hair. "I'm sorry," she said, her laughter growing in intensity as she combed her fingers through his curls.

"No, do not be sorry." Henry gave a mischievous smile of his own, leaning in to kiss her lips one more time. "That is something you must never apologize for."

Epilogue

ONE YEAR LATER

Brighton, with all its pebbled beaches and clear summer skies, had never been more beautiful than it was that day. Eleanor sat beside Arthur in the carriage, with Henry on the seat across from them, holding their newborn baby, Leah, as she slept, rocked to sleep by the gentle movement of the carriage over the smooth Brighton roads. They were on their way to Margaret and Lord Hove's wedding, and Eleanor was eager to have everyone meet their little girl.

"Where is the church, Papa?" Arthur asked, craning his neck to see out the window.

"We are nearly there," Henry said.

Arthur slumped back against the cushions, a scowl marking his forehead, his large eyes casting downward in disappointment. "But we have been traveling for a very long time."

"It has only been twenty minutes," Henry said in a teasing voice.

Eleanor hoped Arthur would learn to emulate Henry's patience, but he was always particularly impatient when he was forced to wait to see his cousins in Brighton.

"You cannot play with Ella and Oliver until the wedding is over," Eleanor reminded him.

Arthur sighed quietly, staring intently out the window. "I do not wike weddings."

"Margaret may share some of her wedding cake with you," Eleanor said. Arthur glanced away from the window, his head tipping slightly to the side.

Henry's gaze jumped to Eleanor, his eyes dancing with laughter. "Yes," Henry added. "It will be a delicious fruit cake with almond icing."

Arthur's eyes widened slightly, though he tried to appear nonchalant. Henry rocked Leah as she began to stir, grinning across the carriage at Eleanor. He knew as well as she did that Arthur loved cake of any sort. They had often bargained with Arthur at the dinner table that he could not have his cake if he did not first eat the rest of his meal. Only recently had they discovered that he had been passing his roasted vegetables under the table to his cat.

"Perhaps if you are well behaved, Lord Hove will give you one of the candies he keeps in his waistcoat pocket," Eleanor said.

Arthur grimaced, sticking out his tongue. "I don't wike those candies."

Henry chuckled quietly. "Why ever not? They may have been in his pocket since his yellow waistcoat was sewn, years and years ago."

Eleanor stifled her laughter for Arthur's sake, throwing

Henry a berating glance for teasing him so mercilessly. She sighed with contentment. She was so happy for Margaret and Lord Hove, their unique qualities and personalities perfectly suited to one another. And above all, they both shared an abiding love of well-polished canes.

She and Henry were well-suited for other reasons, many that she was still discovering with each day that passed. Above all, they both shared an abiding love for Arthur, for their little Leah, and for each other, and that was all she could ever want.

Find the complete series on Amazon

Brides of Brighton

A CONVENIENT ENGAGEMENT

MARRYING MISS MILTON

ROMANCING LORD RAMSBURY

MISS WESTON'S WAGER

AN UNEXPECTED BRIDE

About the Author

Ashtyn Newbold grew up with a love of stories. When she discovered chick flicks and Jane Austen books in high school, she learned she was a sucker for romantic ones. When not indulging in sweet romantic comedies and regency period novels (and cookies), she writes romantic stories of her own across several genres. Ashtyn also enjoys baking, singing, sewing, and anything that involves creativity and imagination.

www.ashtynnewbold.com

Printed in Great Britain
by Amazon